W9-AVR-363

BURGER WUSS

· · · · · · · · · · ·

M. T. ANDERSON

CANDLEWICK PRESS

To L.B.A., my little sister

Copyright © 1999 by M. T. Anderson

First paperback edition in this format 2008

The Library of Congress has cataloged the hardcover edition as follows:

Anderson, Matthew T.

Burger Wuss / M. T. Anderson. — 1st ed.

p.   cm.

Summary: Hoping to lose his loser image, Anthony plans revenge on
a bully which results in a war between two competing fast-food
restaurants, Burger Queen and O'Dermott's.

ISBN 978-0-7636-0680-0 (hardcover)

[1. Fast-food restaurants—Fiction. 2. Restaurants—Fiction.
3. Self-acceptance—Fiction. 4. Bullies—Fiction.
5. Humorous stories.]   I. Title.

PZ7.A5446Bu 1999

[Fic]—dc21   99-14257

ISBN 978-0-7636-1567-3 (first paperback edition)
ISBN 978-0-7636-3178-9 (reformatted paperback)

16 17 18 19 20 21 22 RRC 11 10 9 8 7 6 5 4

Printed in Crawfordsville, IN, U.S.A.

This book was typeset in Baskerville.

Candlewick Press
99 Dover Street
Somerville, Massachusetts 02144

visit us at www.candlewick.com

Chapter 1

. . . .

I told them I was there for the interview. A beeper went off. For a second, the girl stared at me. The beeper was still going off. "That's the quality control beeper," she explained. "I'll go get Mike. He talks to people about working. Excuse me." She turned around. I smiled in a secret way. I thought, *They will suspect nothing. I look as calm and normal as can be.*

Mike was the manager. He wore blue, and everyone else wore green. He seemed very friendly and held out his hand. I shook it. He said, "I'm Mike. Nice to meet you. You're Anthony?"

I said, "Yes. It's nice to meet you, too."

He said, "Let's sit down. Would you like a shake?" We walked out into the dining area. He said, "Now to talk, would you prefer a booth or a free-standing table?"

I shrugged. I said, "Booth, I guess."

He grinned. "Good!" he said. "That will be fine!"

We sat down at a booth. I carefully put my hands on my lap. Over my head was a cardboard mobile of

Kermit O'Dermott, an elf who talked to hamburgers. The sun was coming through the windows and searing the tile floor and the plastic vines and rhododendrons.

I said, "It looks very cheerful in here today."

He said, "Isn't it nice? Corporate Headquarters just sent us some new signage. It's very effective, don't you think? Now." He had a clipboard with him. My application was on it. I felt very nervous. I thought to myself, *Green sateen. Green sateen.* I thought this for private reasons. There are times when you have to hide what you're really up to.

I said, "So." The cardboard Kermit O'Dermott was playing his magical harp. In commercials, it made beverages dance.

He said, "So. Could you tell me some things you could say about yourself?"

"Yes," I said. "I could tell you I'm sixteen—"

"Can you drive?"

"Yes," I said, "but I don't have a car. I can walk here from home."

"Do you have any previous work experience?"

"Yes," I said. "I had a paper route for three years. I know that isn't making burgers or anything, but, you know . . ."

He was looking out the window over my shoulder. There was a Kermit O'Dermott–themed jungle gym out there, and some kids were playing on it. He turned back to me and grinned. He said, "Good, good. The reason you would like to work at O'Dermott's? Just a few words."

I could not tell him the real reason. I had prepared a

clever and cheerful-sounding fake reason. I told him, "I really like people. I like meeting people and I like talking with them. People are so different, and it's great to see people from all over. In a job like this, I would get to see all sorts of people that I couldn't see otherwise. Maybe I'd learn something about people that I can't even know yet."

He laughed. "That's the spirit!" he said. "We work as a team here. We even play as a team." He looked out the window again at the kids on the jungle gym. "That's how it is. Should kids be doing that?"

I turned around and looked out the window. I shrugged. I said, "I think kids pretty much always hit each other like that."

He said, "Little kids' skulls are really soft, though. You don't know that until you have your own kids. My wife just had kids."

"Oh," I said. "More than one?"

He said, "Two. Twins. Two twins."

I said, "I think the skull thickens after a few months or something."

He said, "Well, Anthony, it just so happens that we have a position open at the moment. Do you know Diana Gritt? She also goes to Taft High. She just quit and left a cashier position open."

I rubbed my knees with my fingertips. I considered evil. I thought, *Green sateen. Green sateen.* I said, "Oh, yeah? I know Diana Gritt."

He said, "Small world. I have a few more interviews this week, but I should be able to call you back pretty quick."

I said, "Really? That would be great."

He said, "Great. Now let's talk about hours."

Through the plastic undergrowth I could see Turner come out of the back, dressed in green. I watched him. Turner was the reason I was there. Turner and anger. He stood behind his register. He ran his hand over his greasy blond crew cut. Mike and I talked about hours. I saw Turner see me. I thought that suddenly he had an ugly look on his face. He shook his head. I laughed to myself and looked again. Now I couldn't tell if he had recognized me. I thought maybe the ugly look had just been him cleaning his molars with his tongue. Maybe he had not recognized me at all.

Mike and I were done with the interview. We stood up to shake hands. I banged my knee on the table. I hunched over. When I swore, it was quietly. Mike reached out to give me a hand. I tried to smile. I was bent over a little. I rubbed the knee. Mike was saying, "We are part of a team here. I hope you'll become part of our team. I think you'll really like it here."

He turned and walked toward the counter. Turner faced the other way. Before I left, I stood for a moment. I thought, *Green sateen,* and stared at him. I stared at his back. His neck was a boiled red. We stood there for a long time like that before I left.

Some paramedics were ordering Happy Lunches. Maybe for someone else. They pointed at the board. They specified their prizes.

· · ·

The next day, I met my friends Rick and Jenn at the mall. We met in the food court. There was a Wendy's, an Au Bon Pain, and a Happy Wok. All the seats and tables were fixed to the floor. We watched kids we knew from school mop and daub. They were uniformed in red.

Jenn and Rick both worked at O'Dermott's. Jenn was taller than Rick. Rick was more muscular than Jenn. They were in love. They were holding hands.

"Hey, Anthony," said Rick.

"Hi, Anthony," said Jenn.

I said, "Hi, Jenn, Rick. Hey."

We looked around. I said, "So what's up?"

Rick said, "Basically, dog bites water."

Jenn nodded in agreement.

I said, "Sure. *Dog bites water?*"

Rick and Jenn looked at each other and smiled. They sighed. Rick looked at me and explained kindly, "When there's no news, the newspaper always runs a picture of like three kids playing with a fire hydrant and a dog biting water."

"I see. And I was supposed to get that?"

Since they started going out Rick and Jenn had kind of become their own little nation, with its own special language.

"Well, there's not much news," said Rick.

"Rick's older brother won't get out of the bathtub," Jenn offered. "He thinks everything is unclean."

"Man," I said.

"Yeah," said Rick. "He's wearing down his loofah."

"Is he okay?" I asked. "I mean, like: okay?"

Rick looked a little uneasy. He said, "I don't think so. He cries the whole time."

We all looked at our feet. Rick's brother was usually normal. He had a straight B average. We were quiet.

"Here's news," I said. "I applied to O'Dermott's."

"No way!" said Rick.

"That would be so chow if you were there!" said Jenn.

"You know," said Rick, "Diana quit. Last week."

"So you told me," I said.

"You have all this stuff to look forward to!" said Jenn. "Like the worst are the guys from the computer company who come in at lunch and go, 'You know, you could increase efficiency if you like reorganized around a different networking principle,' and it's like, 'Okay, I'm just a cashier here, but no, please, why don't I during my lunch break just reorganize the whole company, sure, thanks buddy, thanks for all the genius.'"

"No," said Rick. "The worst is like the senior citizens that keep coming back for free coffee and then sit around swearing and groping the employees."

"No," said Jenn. "The worst is like that woman, the Iced Tea Lady, who orders like four large iced teas and then when you go into the bathroom later it's—"

"No," said Rick, "or the guy who can't—"

"The unsalted man?"

"Yeah, who like—"

"Oh, God, he's the worst! He really is!"

"Every Thursday!"

They grabbed hands and screamed in high-pitched voices into each other's faces.

"So I have all that to look forward to," I said.

"Yes," said Jenn.

"Too crew," said Rick. I didn't know what he meant, but I let it slide.

"*If* you get the job," said Jenn. "It's pretty competitive."

I gave her a look. "What?" I said. "Are you saying I'm not qualified?"

"No, man," said Rick. "But not everyone can get a job."

I said, "Because I think I'm qualified to work at O'Dermott's, thanks."

"Calm," said Rick. "Calm. It's great you've applied. We'd love to have you."

"Better O'Dermott's than Burger Queen," said Jenn. "They are all a mass of shame at BQ. They just got a condiment troll."

"What's a condiment troll?" I asked.

"A four-and-a-half-foot plastic troll that dispenses ketchup and mustard," answered Rick. "It's a promotional item."

"They should just hide their faces in their paper crowns," said Jenn.

"But good luck," said Rick. "Really. That'll be jump if you end up at OD's."

"Jump," I said. "Yeah."

It was evening. My father was sitting on the kitchen counter, talking to my mother. I was walking up and down the stairs for exercise. I was improving my calves and hams. The telephone rang. I had just reached the landing for the twenty-fourth time.

My mother called up to me, "It's Mike from O'Dermott's."

I went down and got the phone. I took it into the living room. It was portable, so I could also hear WMTA and Mrs. Gravitz from next door.

"Hi," I said. "This is Anthony."

"That's the neighbor's boy," said Mrs. Gravitz distantly to her daughter. They kept up their conversation in a mumble.

Through the static, Mike said, "Hi, Anthony. I'm calling to say you got the job."

"That's great!" I said. "I'm really looking forward to this."

"We're glad to have you as part of the O'Dermott's team."

I wanted to make a good impression. I said, "I, like I'm so glad to be part of it. I wouldn't want to be at Burger Queen. Have you heard, they just got some kind of . . . have you heard about their troll?"

There was a silence. Mrs. Gravitz buzzed like locusts.

Mike said, "Troll? I don't know about a troll."

I said quickly, "Their troll . . . with ketchup?"

"Oh," said Mike. "That's what we call in the business a promotional condiment dump. It's a fine piece."

"Oh," I said. "Okay."

"Well, Anthony. Why don't you come by at two on Saturday? Then you can undergo trainage."

So that was it. I wrote down the time on a pad and

read it back to him. I didn't want to make any mistakes. Mrs. Gravitz said she'd remind me.

It was a good thing that Mike—or anyone else empowered to make hiring decisions—could not look inside my mind. The day I found out about my rosy O'Dermott's future, my head was going a mile a minute. A psychic Mike might have detected a certain strangeness. It was good he could not read my thoughts. I paced in my room. I had decided it was important to hide any outward signs that might make people like him suspicious. That was part of my scheme. I was just pacing. Nothing strange about that. I guess my teeth were sort of grinding. And when I got particularly angry, I caught myself making a kind of barking sound. I kicked the furniture a little. I occasionally pounded on the desk and cried, "Why, why, *why?*" But otherwise, outwardly calm. And this is what I thought:

Okay so I am angry, okay so I am not thinking very logically, but the time is past for being logical, and now it's high time for no more Mr. Nice Guy. Being Mr. Nice Guy got me exactly jack, I can tell you—everyone saying I'm such a sweet kid, it got me nothing but screwed over, and I mean big time. It's time to drop-kick nice. Forget it. What I need now is revenge, and revenge is what I'm going to get—yes! What I really need is a plan.

She is wonderful for so many reasons, and luck, you bet it was luck to have her fall in love with me in the first place, considering who I am, which is not anyone much, being that I don't have many friends and am thought a freak by what I guess are all and sundry. But I have a heart and yes I loved her and the reasons just started with these:

☞ She was so beautiful when I first saw her: dressed all in green like an elf of the forest, as if she should have been playing a mandolin, perching in an apple tree, her uniform as she bagged my fries sparkling in the light, and as I said to her, looking at the smoothness of her face, "I have exact change," the smell of the burgers wafted across us like strands of her flaxen hair in mountain winds.

☞ She was haughty for some time, by which I mean she didn't pay any attention to me when we passed in the halls, which is not surprising because I am not anybody, I mean not one of the rich or the handsome or the pierced or the shaved—and her not recognizing me in the hall, which I guess made sense, seeing that our only conversation had been about

     — a Big O sandwich
     — six piece nuggets
     — small fries
     — medium chocolate shake
     — (exact change)

her not recognizing me in the hall, as I said, made me want to speak to her even more, so that after the talent show, when everybody finally saw me and knew what I really could do and what I had inside me, when she came over and complimented me on my act as The Laughing Contortionist, I actually had the spit and guts to ask her out on a date, which we went on, and she said I was a riot and we had like this great time and pizza.

☞ She had like the most beautiful smile. It was perfect in every way. It lit up the whole of her face and made her cheeks to dimples.

☞ None of her teeth were hers. The real ones were knocked out on some steps several years ago. The guy got away with her wallet and her mother's purse. All of the new teeth were made of an unusual and sexy plastic polymer. I am telling you, those new teeth were perfect in every way.

☞ She had an enormous appetite. She was not a very large girl but she could put away a very large pizza. I am telling you, she ate with gusto. At first we were going slice for slice, and then she started lapping me, and soon I had all this admiration for her like when cowboys meet a dame who can not only hold shots of tequila better than they can but can eat the dead worm too.

• • •

Being around her can be summed up like this: She convinced me to do things I never would have done. When I think about my life before I met her it's mostly a landscape of video games, movies, hanging out, eating chips, not buying things, saying, "What's up?" saying, "Nothing," saying, "Yeah, man," and going on the occasional incompetent high-impact sports spree with Rick, for instance the homemade bungee jump we named "Mother's Tears."

Before her, my life was dull, and I knew I was safe, safe, safe. I was going crazy, things were so safe. I would look out the window on hot nights and know, *out there, people are living.* By living I guess I meant making out and cow-tipping. I would be like, *I am trapped in here, in my own safe little life, but I am a teenager and this is supposed to be the time when I am really living,* and I would pace in circles trapped inside the house, and drink all of the orange juice, and pace some more thinking about popular kids in fast cars, and I'd go to the basement and turn on the Game-Brat and wallop orcs until the screen was green with blood.

But she changed all that. I had this suspicion that she lived whatever life she wanted to. I knew she hung out with the kids who all the gossip was about. The good-looking kids. The kids who laughed in the halls. I imagined the parties, the ski trips, the beach runs. I wanted unusual things to happen to me. I was a little afraid of her, because I thought they were already happening to her. I thought I was too nice. Too quiet. Too shy.

The second time we went on a date, we were driving home from the mall, and I was frightened by her, and I was wondering how I was going to bring up the subject of Am I allowed to kiss you?, when she told me to pull over, and I saw some kids vandalizing a sign, and I thought, *No way am I pulling over,* but she said, "Pull over," and I didn't want to seem like I was afraid when she wasn't, so I pulled over.

I shouldn't have worried, because they were just these kids who had been going around town correcting all the grammatical errors on signs, which Diana thought was hilarious. When we stopped them, they were working on:

DRIVE
SLOW︿ly

Diana talked to them. She was so enthusiastic about their work on the posters for Berringer's Contact Lense Bananza that they let us travel around with them that night, let us take them from place to place in my parents' car, the four of them in the back seat (they were skinny) and the two of us up front, which was an adventure, and was amazing, except that one of them licked the velour armrest just to be freaky. We drove around and told jokes and laughed. The moon was out. When we stopped, we could hear rodents in the grass and bushes. We were doing what they called a major strike, which meant going around the town border to every sign that said "Billingston:

A Great Place to Live In," and fixing what they called its dangling preposition. We'd pull over, get out. There'd be the rattle of the ball in the spray can, then the cool hiss, the look of cross-eyed attention on their scrawny faces, and then the can lids being popped back on. Presto:

Billingston:
A Great Place ^to Live ~~In~~
in which

I thought at first that Diana knew them, but it turned out she didn't, she had just heard about them, and we had both seen them around at school but hadn't noticed them, because they were just four more skinny kids in plaid shirts, but Diana was so amazing that it was like she had always known them. She laughed at all their jokes and when I was driving them around I would turn my head quickly to catch a glimpse of her, and she would be looking at me in this way, like she was admiring me for driving them. I was shy with all of them around. I was quiet. But her eyes were friendly when she looked at me.

They asked me to drive over to the town forest. I did whatever they said. It was on the other side of town. Our windows were open, and we could smell the wet hay. It was so sweet it was stuffy.

At the entrance to the town forest, there was a parking area for the ski and hiking trails. They told me to park there. I did.

We walked into the woods. We could see every-thing that night, because of the moon. One of them had seen some bad grammar in the woods a few days before. We had to walk about a mile to get to the grammar. Diana and I were walking in the middle of them. They were all around us, reciting the dialogue from a Japanese cartoon. They knew it all by heart. I guess it had been dubbed, because when they recited it, they moved their mouths even when they weren't talking. I asked how far we were going. One of them said, "We're almost there." We kept on walking.

In the woods was a giant concrete wall. I don't know what it protected. Something governmental, I guess. One of the four said, "There it is." It was in blue spray paint. It said:

Guy's Suck

They all started laughing. They slapped each other on the shoulder blades. They slapped us. I thought they were going to choke. "An apostrophe! An apos-trophe! Oh, that's rich! . . . Like it . . . ha ha ha ha ha! . . . like it . . . ha ha ha ha! . . . takes the genitive!" Two of them fell on the ground.

Diana and I had to stand against the wall, side by side, while two of them climbed up on us to reach the apostrophe. They sprayed it out. I could feel Diana's shoulder against mine. She wiggled it. Her arms were bare. I couldn't tell if she was trying to get closer to me or trying to get farther away so we wouldn't touch. I thought about saying something to her, about how close we were. I guess it wasn't a very good moment, though. There was a rotting sneaker (size ten) on either side of my head. That's not a romantic thing for people.

Walking back through the forest, Diana and I fell behind. They were ahead, reciting comedy sketches in some kind of Viking accent. We could see their long, thin bodies hopping all over the path.

I said, "I'm glad we did this. For me, this is adventure."

She said, "It is for me, too. I never do this kind of thing."

"That's—I mean, I'm surprised. I thought you did this kind of thing all the time."

She said, "I don't go out much."

"What about with all those kids you hang out with? Jeff and Sue and Mark and stuff?"

"No. They get boring fast. Really fast. All they care about are their cars and their beach parties. I'm like, is this all there is to life? Some day I want to be out there, really *living*."

Diana and I were walking side by side. The pine woods were darker than the rest of the forest. It didn't make any sense not to touch her. I thought she probably wanted me to make a move. I thought she was waiting.

I am not sure what it is that finally allows people to just turn to each other and touch. There is some hidden trigger. There is a secret language people learn, so they can signal to stop talking and just move. I don't know it.

So instead I kept talking. I said, "I always thought you were someone things happened to."

"What sorts of things?"

"You know. I thought you led a life of risk and adventure."

She shrugged. "Here's what I know: People will think that, if you have a certain kind of hair."

My brain was racing. I was thinking of her in a new way. I was trying to picture her as being this person who longed for some adventure, just like me, and now I really wanted to kiss her, especially because it seemed like she might be lagging behind with me on purpose. The idea that she might be thinking about me and how she wanted to kiss my face, my face behind which was a brain wanting to kiss hers—I am telling you, that idea was like this new force of gravity pulling me silently toward her like in an asteroid disaster film where there's an asteroid flying around at a billion miles an hour and of all the places it could go in outer space like

— the Rings of Jupiter
— Alpha Centauri
— the Horse Head Nebula

it is instead headed right for the corner of Broadway and Fourth.

"It's a beautiful night," she said.

"Yes," I replied. "The interstate sounds like a mountain stream."

Now I was in a panic. I knew there was a good chance that we both wanted to kiss, but I didn't know how to say it. I couldn't just say some sleazy line like, "Do you want to make out now?" because I didn't want to be one of those baconheads who force themselves on girls. On the other hand, I thought, at least those baconheads get what they want—but no, I thought, I am too much Mr. Nice Guy, and plus who wants to kiss someone and have her say something like "Plluugh!" and wipe her mouth with the back of her hand? I didn't want to be like one of those guys you see in the city who yells after strange women, "Hey baby! I'll be thinking about you to-*NIGHT!*" and you think, *You know, buddy, there's a reason you'll only be thinking.* So I guess what I'm saying is that I was really liking her, and I didn't want to disgust her, but I couldn't just do nothing, because doing nothing either was pathetic and I was Pathetic Boy, or it was kind of gross and I was like a lurker, you know, wearing a trench coat and stealing women's addresses, building shrines of hair clippings, and following them in an unmarked forklift. . . .

So I decided to play it safe and say that we were falling behind and we should catch up. Then we'd move up and be with the rest of them. She would never have to know what I was thinking in the secrecy of my brain.

"We're falling behind," I said. "We should catch up."

She stopped. We were standing in a rut. She said, "Don't you want to be the kind of person things happen to?"

I can't remember how we started kissing then. I can't remember who moved first. I can't remember a thing.

I just remember hearing the footsteps ahead of us stop. Hearing them turn. Hearing them yell, "THE KIND OF PERSON *TO WHOM* THINGS— whoops. Hot damn."

That was a few months ago, just before school got out. For the next two months, we had a great time together. We went through automatic car washes relentlessly and were sarcastic for hours at Toys "R" Us. We hung out after school and I went over to her house and she came over to my house and we watched movies about alien intestinal viruses and commandoes on golf carts.

One day I took her canoeing—can you believe it? canoeing?—I took her canoeing like Mr. Wholesome and we went down the river and behind the orchard, and crept up the bank inside the fence and stole apples, lots of them, filling the fronts of our shirts with them, and when our shirts were filled, I could see her belly and her bellybutton underneath all the apples, and even the soft line of her lowest rib, and we carried our apples back to my parents' canoe and dumped them in, and then I was going to kiss her, until the man in the plaid shirt started to throw rocks, and pushing off became a really really good idea.

For once I was doing things with people other than Rick, and my parents stopped hovering over me and asking me, "Do you have any friends? Do you have any friends?" because she was not just my girlfriend, she was my friend, and she came over and actually talked to my parents sometimes, and made them laugh too, and then, when she left, my parents would say, "She's such a great girl!" which is like completely embarrassing but is better than them saying, "Why don't you go out and try to meet some young women at the Bowl-O-Drome?"

Well, all I'm trying to say is that it was great being with her, and everything seemed perfect to me. Everything was like an adventure.

She said that the next summer we should hike part of the Appalachian Trail together. I suggested we bike it on Big Wheels. This was something we looked into. It excited both of us.

She was smart. She was sure of herself. She knew when it was getting boring to be cheerful. She had a sense of humor that was quick and harsh and which always surprised me, for example now I remember her saying that she was sick of the O'Dermott's Happy Lunch, man, and wasn't it about time to deal with reality and do the Desolate Lunch instead, with games on the box like "Can you help Kermit get to safety?" and the answer is "No," and "Can you find these words in the puzzle?" and the answer is "No," and "Can you connect the dots?" and the answer is "No," and "Can you tell three things wrong with this picture?" and the answer is "No," and inside for a prize there is broken things or dust.

I guess I could not tell what was wrong with the picture. Diana didn't say anything, so I couldn't know, and maybe she didn't know either, and so I went to the party with the others, and was standing there, and we danced for a while, with me doing one of my extra-funny Laughing Contortionist dances, but that night no one really thought it was funny. People were serious that night about getting drunk and the music was serious. The beat was strong and the rugs were rolled back. She kept on talking to people I didn't know. She didn't introduce me. Finally, I couldn't find her.

I was drunk, which, being that I don't have much body weight, means I'd swigged two beers and was already more looney-tunes than Porky, and the point is I was not having fun and I wanted to see her. I went around from room to room. Rick and Jenn walked around with me. They said things to each other like, "Hey, Jenny Jujube," and "Hey, Tricky Ricky," and "Hey, Jenny Gin Mill," and "Maybe Diana's like gone milk carton. Remember? Milk carton? Missing?" We looked for Diana high and low.

I did not know Turner at that point, so I did not recognize him when I found him on top of her on a sofa. They had some of their clothes on. A few. She had his green sateen O'Dermott's jacket around her shoulders. She was laughing at something. She was very drunk.

Rick said, "She's in here. Horizontal."

"Shouldn't they be standing up to talk?" Jenn said.

Rick said, "He just bit her lip."

Rick and Jenn turned away. They patted me on

the shoulder as they walked back past me and left me there.

I felt like I was standing on the last tip of something big that was sinking—didn't know what to do. Stood by the door. She hadn't seen me. Go up? Jab him? Yell and punch? Yell and wait for him to get up? Take it outside? Right here? Let her go? Say something short, something quick, something hard that would hurt, say it and turn and leave, sneer in the halls? There were no swearwords dark enough, nothing cutting enough—because I wanted words then to cut, and thinking this now, and remembering his green sateen jacket draped around her shaking shoulders, I want that again, want my thoughts to be a blade, my brains to detonate, to punch, to scream, to find some way to hurt.

So I ran away. I turned around and started to run out of the house. She saw, called after me, "Wait—omigod!—Anthony! Wait! I'm sorry!" I stopped and waited. I went back a few steps. I was in the shadows. Turner was sitting up now. He was very tall and wide. He had lifted up one hand, with two fingers raised limply to caution her. He was saying, "Shh! Shh!" He waited. He said, "I think he's gone."

She covered her eyes with her hand. She said, "Oh God. I'll have to talk to him tomorrow. Oh man. What a mess."

Turner said, "Don't sweat it. He's a little wuss."

She said, "Yeah, but he's really nice. You're sitting on my leg."

Turner said, "Bendy-boy's a little wuss. He ran away."

She said, "You're sitting on my leg. He's really nice."

I was glad I was really nice. It was really nice to be really nice. I walked outside. Jenn and Rick were tagging after me. They were saying how sorry they were. They said that, man, they couldn't believe her. They said she obviously didn't understand about love.

I heard Rick whisper, "That wasn't her green sateen jacket, was it?"

Jenn whispered back, "Would you call that green or loden?"

They both started to giggle but then Rick said, "Shh, he's really messed up." They said that wow, like what was I going to do? They said they didn't know what they'd do if they were me. They said bye. I walked home. On the way I punched an oak. An oak. I didn't punch him, I punched an oak. It really hurt my knuckles.

I couldn't go to bed. I wouldn't be able to go to sleep. I paced in my room. The next morning, I called Rick, who ever since he and Jenn realized one night that they were more than just friends had been the guru of love. I found out about Turner. He just graduated from high school in the next town over. He's going away to college. He works with her at O'Dermott's. He goes out with a lot of girls. They say his appeal is that he's handsome and dangerous. He always seems to know what he's doing. Guys respect him. He's six-two. He goes by his last name.

She called me later that morning. My mother was glad to hear her on the phone. I could hear my mother say, "Oh hi, Diana! It's great to hear from you! How are you these days? I bought some more cheese popcorn for the next time you come over." I was in the bathroom, looking at myself in the mirror and wondering why I was so damn ugly. I thought about avoiding her, but I went and took it. My parents were standing by, listening and smiling like: "Ah, young love!"

I said, "Hi." Flatly.

She said, "Hi. Anthony, I feel really bad." Sheepishly.

I said, "I feel pretty bad too." I wanted that to be coldly, but it sounded just like I was sorry for something I'd done. I hadn't done anything.

"Anthony, just, we were drinking, and like there was this chemistry. I couldn't . . ."

"Chemistry," I said. "Just this chemistry."

"I couldn't help it."

I said, "I was working in the lab, late one night."

She said, "Anthony."

I said, "When my eyes beheld a fearful sight."

"Anthony, please don't do this. God, I can't believe you're doing this."

My parents were laughing. They had big grins like: "Our son the riot!"

My father started singing. "Oh the monster from his slab began to rise, and suddenly, before my eyes . . ."

"Diana—" I said. I felt sick. I turned away from my parents into the corner of the room. Their shadows were cast across me. They were dancing. They did the monster mash.

She was saying, "Look, Anthony, it's better this way. It wasn't really working out anyway. I mean, I really like you and all, but I think it's better—"

My parents sang, "The Monster Mash!"—"It was a graveyard smash!"—"The Monster Mash!"—"It caught on in a flash. . . ."

She was saying, "Is that your parents singing?"

"Diana—please, Diana—" I said. I thought of her bellybutton in the sunlight, of her lying with the green sateen jacket around her shoulders, of her lying with Turner on top of her; I was almost crying.

"I really think it's better we just be friends."

"Vutever happened to my Transylvania tvist?"

"Why not working out?" I said. "Diana, I really like you."

"No, don't think I didn't have a good time. Because I had a really good time. All the time."

My parents were watching me. They were quieting down. They weren't dancing anymore. I tried to be cool on the phone. I controlled my voice. I said, "Why don't we go out for lunch?"

My father said, "You can take the car. I don't need it!"

She said, "I don't think we should. Can we just put this whole thing behind us? Not hurt anyone's feelings?"

I couldn't answer with my parents watching. They were listening to every word. So instead I said cheerily, "I'll just drop it off at your work. Is that okay?"

She said, "What? Anthony, what are you talking about?"

I said, "No, thanks, I'm done with it. Turned out I didn't need it. I'll just drop it off at your work."

"What are you—?"

I laughed what was supposed to be a cheerful laugh, but it was a cackle. "Oh, ho ho ho! In Magic Marker, too? All over the shackles?"

"Would you be serious? I'm trying to be serious."

I chuckled. "In the seventh level of hell, they're all upside down in dung!"

"Fine," she said. "Fine. This is exactly what I'm talking about." And she slammed down the phone. I waited for a second. There was a dial tone.

"Good then," I said. "I'll drop it by sometime today or maybe tomorrow. Love ya!"

I grinned a big grin and hung up the phone. My parents were smiling like: "You two—so sweet!"

I went back upstairs to look at myself in the mirror and figure out what made me so ugly.

That same afternoon Turner made fun of Diana at work. I don't know what he said, because I wasn't there, but he at first just was polite but sort of ignoring her, and then later after she kept on saying, "Are we going to talk? Staff room. Now!" he got mean, and made some comment about them making out and nice extra-value meals, I don't know exactly because Rick and Jenn weren't listening carefully (they were cowering and holding hands behind the shake machine until things blew over), but Turner said terrible things, and Diana started crying, and she threw down her visor, and she quit.

I called Diana later. She had her own line. She was screening. I left messages. She never returned them.

Now it's been a week since the party. A week since I found Turner lying on top of her, almost undressed. I am going to get revenge. I hate him and his green sateen. I will go to any length. Whatever it takes to make him hurt. I want to see him cry.

I am starting to smolder now. No more Mr. Nice Guy. No more Mr. Wholesome. I will crawl through sewers, knife in teeth. Climb up walls with suction boots. Nurse my hatred like a baby with pincer hands and twelve legs. I will get revenge. I will make a plan. I will do what I need to.

I will have it my way.

Chapter 2

. . . .

Now is the time to be scheming and like evil, I thought to myself. *Now for revenge.* I smiled cruelly to myself. I practiced several times. You have to narrow your eyes and only curl one half of the mouth. The video said, "Double-fold the bag. Extend it toward the customer. Say, 'Thank you. Have a nice day!' This closes the transaction. Remember, a friendly face is the key to a friendly customer and customer satisfaction."

I practiced my venomous glare.

The video screen went blank. The introduction was over. I sat in the dark staff room. I tried a vicious laugh.

"Eh he he he he he he!" I tried it more from the belly. "Oh eh heh heh heh heh heh!"

"Anthony, hello?" Mike looked in.

I stopped laughing.

"You done with the footage?"

"Yes," I said. "I think I've got it."

He turned on the lights. He said he would give me a tour of the restaurant.

We walked out of the staff room. He introduced me to one of the cooks.

"Here's one of our cooks."

There was a kid I thought I had seen around at school. He had shaved all his hair down to a faint golden fuzz. He said, "I'm Shunt. Welcome to corporate hell. Start screaming now."

Mike said, "Shunt is a real individual. He's an unusual member of our O'Dermott's family."

Shunt said, "He grill or register?"

Mike said, "Register. You need someone for grill?"

Shunt said, "No. Just asking is all." He kept on walking.

Mike showed me the deep-freeze locker. He showed me how to get out from the inside. He showed me where the janitorial supplies were kept. We went to the inside of Drive-Thru Window Number One. No one was there. It was a slow time. He showed me the office. There was a corkboard covered with Instamatic photos. They were all of the O'Dermott's softball team winning against the Burger Queen team. It looked like it had been quite a day.

Mike said, "If you have any questions, I'll ask Turner to take care of you. He'll be overseeing you. You know Turner?"

I stuttered with surprise. Then I thought, *Don't panic. Don't panic! This will be perfect. I'll be close to him. This will be absolutely perfect for me to hatch a plan.*

I said mysteriously, "Turner and I go way back."

"Good!" Mike said.

Mike and I passed the grills and vats. Shunt was there.

Mike said, "This is where all the burgers are cooked and dressed."

Shunt said to me as he worked, "There are thirteen layers in a Big O: top bun, onions, meat, pickles, lettuce, Super Sauce, middle bun, onions, meat, cheese, lettuce, Super Sauce, bottom bun. In this stack, we're the meat. These patties are made of our expended brains, nerves, and muscle."

Mike said, "You see the humorous way Shunt looks at the world?"

We went to the registers. Mike said, "You'll be working a register. At the beginning of your shift, you get a drawer. We know how much money is in your drawer. Be careful when you give people change. We count up how much you have at the end of your shift. Any shortage or overage and we write it down. You get a shortage or overage above ten dollars each shift for a week and you're fired. Okay? Let's go talk to Turner."

Mike led me over to Turner. He said, "Turner's an old pro. You know Anthony?"

I glared at Turner. I smiled like his archenemy. I folded my hands slowly in front of my green polyester smock.

Turner looked at me blankly. "No," he said. "I don't think we've met." He held out his hand. "I'm Turner."

I raised my eyebrows harshly. I said, "I think we met the other night."

He thought. "No," he said, shaking his head.

"We met at a party. Remember?"

He looked at the ceiling and thought. "Nope," he said.

Mike looked at me strangely.

I said, "Oh."

I was a little surprised by this. But then I thought, *This will be perfect. No problem at all. Yes, perfect. He won't suspect a thing. So, Mr. Turner. You are defenseless.*

"Sometimes I'm not around. Turner will answer your questions. Turner's a shift supervisor and one of our star employees. Anyone can progress in our organization if they just give us their all. Turner did, and he just bought a car with his earnings, didn't you?"

"That's right, Mike. Her name is Margot."

"He also earned a green O'Dermott's jacket for outside wear."

"I've seen those O'Dermott's jackets," I said. "Yes, I've seen them. That's a very handsome style."

"We like to think so. Let's go look at the bathrooms."

Mike and I went down the hall to the bathrooms. We walked out into the main dining area. Mike showed me the jungle gym. We went back behind the counter. Mike showed me Window Number Two. Two workers were staring out of Window Number Two. They were reflected in the glass. Their mouths were both open, like they were dreaming.

I went to one of the registers. I started working. For a while, Mike stayed by my side. He showed me which buttons to press. He reminded me what order I should get things in. He helped me send grill orders back to Shunt.

Shunt was singing a country and western song of his own imagining. It went, "I'm a vegan burger-flipper on minimum wage."

Then Mike went back to the office. Turner was helpful when I had a question. I would ask him, "How do you erase a fries?" He told me. I would say, "Where do I get the apple pies?" He told me that too.

But his kindness did not change how I felt. All I had to do was look at him, and I could picture him lying on top of her with his eyes closed. His eyes had been closed with pleasure. He had really been enjoying himself. I thought of her and how kind she had always been to me. I thought of how much she had laughed at my jokes. I could not believe that Turner knew the taste of her teeth.

That was a taste like no other taste. The tang of thrilling plastic polymers. I remembered a few weeks before, us sitting out in the town forest. We had found a place hidden behind some scrub pine. We could hear the zipping of dirt bikes on the paths. We were kissing.

"Can you taste it in your food?" I asked.

"No," she said. "When you have a taste in your mouth all the time, after a while you can't taste it. Your taste buds rearrange somehow. It's completely normal for me."

I asked, "How can it be a taste if you can't taste it?"

She said, "You know what I mean. I'm sure it's always in there."

"It's a beautiful taste," I said.

She put her hand on the side of my head to steady it, so she could look in my eyes. I watched her mouth and chin. She said, "How does it taste?"

I said, "A little bitter. Like rare Oriental spice."

We kissed again, as dirt bikes hurtled past in groups of three.

"Hey, new boy. Wake up," said Turner. "What's your name again?"

I said, "Anthony. Sorry."

He said, "You like to go out with me and the guys?"

"What guys?"

"Those two clowns," he said, pointing at the two working in the drive-thru window.

"You mean, when our shift is done?"

"Yeah," he said. "Couple of hours from now."

I panicked. I backed away from him a little. But I knew my answer. "Yes. That would be great. I'll go out with you guys."

"Cool," he said, and hit me on the arm. I waited for swelling.

"Where are we going?" I asked.

He said, "Let me make a few calls. We'll plan. Cool."

And so when my shift was over I called my parents and told them I was going out. Turner and the other two guys and I changed out of our uniforms in the bathroom. We still stank like burgers. We walked out into the night smelling like a number three. I guess that was better than smelling like a number two.

Turner's car was in back of the garbage compactor. "Like the ride?" he said, running his hand across the straight lines of the hood. It was an '85 Olds. Every detail had been restored to all its Reagan-era glory. "You like this baby?" He said it like a challenge, like he'd hit me if I said no.

"It's really nice," I said. "It's yours?"

"No one's but me," he said. He unlocked the door. "Paid in cash. This is Margot. She's about fifteen kijillion burgers made into metal." He swung his door open. "Anthony, why don't you sit next to me, up front?"

I got in on the other side. I was terrified. I was twisting my fingers up into knots. The other two got in behind us. "Where we going?" one asked.

"You'll see, boys," said Turner. He had a pack of cigarettes shoved under the sleeve of his T-shirt. He took one out, winked, and lit it. "I think we're in for quite a night."

"Is it down—you know."

"Oh yeah. You got it."

"Out there? Man, is everyone down at the place already?"

"Prob'ly," said Turner. "They've prob'ly already started without us."

"Ah, this is cool," said one of the guys. "You ever done this, kid?"

"What?" I said. I wrapped my thumbs around each other. "What are we doing?"

"It's all the rage," said Turner. He smiled like a wolf, and smoke drizzled out from between his small teeth. "All the rage in the world right now."

He started the car, and screeched out of the parking

lot. I grabbed for my seat belt. We were moving pretty quickly. The businesses on Howett Street and Quell went by, all dark. The two guys in the back were whooping.

"Put on some music," said one. "Put on some tunes!"

"On the radio," said the other. "Or a cassette tape."

"This is all the rage right now," Turner repeated to me. "Everyone's doing it."

"Yeah, man, everyone!" said someone from the back.

I thought, *You will be living the wild life now, man. Now is your chance to learn what makes Turner tick. And to live the wild life. No more Mr. Nice Guy. No more Mr. Wholesome/canoe boy/ good-good/dork. Into the Forbidden Zone.*

The windows were open. We were moving at great speed. The hot summer night blew in. It smelled like lawn clippings from bad and marshy lawns. I could smell the hot metal of passing cars.

"This is the life," said Turner. "I never want to get older." He put on some music. It was a tape of a guitar playing the same note over and over. It was a pretty high note for a guitar, I guess, but not unreasonably high. Turner bobbed his head in time with the note. He sped up, but the note played the same as ever.

"Great stereo," said someone from the back seat. "This a tape?"

We passed kids dawdling by a 7-Eleven. They were not on their skateboards, but were spinning them like tops. We nearly rear-ended a pick-up truck at a stoplight.

"You'll find," said Turner, "that everyone from Burger Queen and Wendy's hangs out with us. We're like one big happy family. Best thing is, it's a chance to meet slim and sexy chiquitas. They don't know what's hit them. You know what I mean?"

"No," I said. I hid the bitterness in my voice. "What do you mean?"

"Stick with me and I'll show you. You kind of a wuss around girls?"

"Yes . . . I mean, no. No." My hands were back to back, with the fingers knotted painfully together. I slumped in my seat.

"Hey, look, buddy," he said, patting me on the shoulder. "It's fine if you are." He laughed loudly. "I mean, the world has to have some wusses. Look, I'll give you a tip when meeting new girls: No does not mean no."

"Sometimes I think girls mean no when no is said."

"And that's where you're wrong, Anthony." He pointed at my nose and jabbed at it with his finger. I flinched. He said, "That's where Anthony is wrong. I think of it like when you're working register: You know, they order a burger and a small fries, and the panel starts flashing drinks, so you go, 'Ma'am, would you like a drink?' It's just like that with girls. Like, you're there, and they've let you put one hand on their leg, the other hand on the back of their neck, and the panel starts flashing, and you go, 'Ma'am, would you like my tongue shoved in your ear?' Always one step further. The hard sell." The two guys in the back laughed and banged the seat-backs.

I wanted to kill him. I separated my hands. I looked at them and thought about how they would look strangling him and starving his ugly little brain of oxygen. I said, "Thanks, Turner. That's a great tip."

"No prob. You ever treated a girl like that? You got to learn. So how was your first day, Anthony?"

I circled the wrist of one hand with fingers from the other. I said, "It was good. I mean, as good as it can be."

Turner looked at me suspiciously. "What do you mean by that?" he asked.

I shrugged. "I mean, as good as it can be, working at O'Dermott's."

He pulled to a halt. He stared.

We sat in the car. The engine still ran. I realized we were at another light. He said, "It's something to be proud of."

I laughed along with the joke. Then I looked at his face. He was not laughing. His eyes were narrow. He was looking at me. I stopped laughing. He said, "Not joking. It's something to be proud of. You're working, kid. We're all working. That's more than some guys can say. Think about that. We're a popular and profitable franchise."

"Yeah," said someone from the back seat. "The man himself is coming at the end of the month."

"Which man?" I said.

"Kermit O'Dermott. On his way here."

I was incredulous. "You mean: the elf?"

Turner nodded with pride. "They're making a commercial at our O'Dermott's. Kermit O'Dermott himself will be there."

Someone from the back said, "They said we could maybe be in it. As extras. And we're going to have a big party."

Turner moved forward. "You got to be proud of your job, man," he said. "There's nothing more American than O'Dermott's. Don't get like Shunt. Man, Shunt's a mess. He has a secret organization. He's trying to destroy O'Dermott's Corporation from the inside. He's a god-damn commie."

One of the guys from the back corrected, "Anarchist."

"Same thing."

"Is not."

"Look," said Turner. "Your like cynicism aside. O'Dermott's is about America. It's about everything that is American." The guitar note pulsed under his speech. He spoke intensely. I thought he was going to cry. "O'Dermott's is about the highway. It's about going places, no time to stop. It's about, 'Go west, young man.' It's like the Pilgrim fathers, wagon trains, the miner forty-niners—"

"The Donner Party," said someone.

"Hey. Hey. I'm serious, pal. We are about a big coun-try. We're about growing. We're about new hope." He pointed at my face. "There has never been a war between two countries with O'Dermott's in them. You know what I'm saying? We," he said, laying his hand on the dashboard, "are the peacemakers."

With that he spun out into the intersection, down old Route 43, past the orchards, past the gravel pits, past the mulch farm, toward our unknown destination. We were moving so fast that the sound of the crickets sawing away in all the fields around us was a single sheet of noise. We were moving so fast I could barely hear dogs' barks rise and fall as we passed houses. They were barking at us because we were on the outside, tearing through town. We were dangerous. We roared through the night.

And then we pulled up to the town's big graveyard. Turner pulled to the side of the road. He stopped the car. Suddenly, he shrieked along with the music, singing, "Dng! Dng! Dng! Dng! Dng! Dng! Dng!" He banged his head in time with the beat. He laughed. He turned off the engine. The tape clicked and stopped.

Through the open windows, we could suddenly hear the individual pulses of the crickets.

He turned around in his seat. "You ready?"

"Yeah."

"Sure thing, Turner."

We got out of the car. We were parked next to a stone wall. We climbed over it, one by one.

"Uh," I said, "about what time will we be finished?"

"Chill out," said Turner. "Depends on how much you can take."

We were walking through the cemetery. The sky was filled with stars. The far horizon was burned orange by the lights of the malls. Everything was still. Small smears of light reflected off dark, slick monuments.

We walked between the oldest stones. They were made of slate. People who had died in the Revolution had little American flags shoved in their plots. I could just barely make out angels and urns.

We passed several crypts. No one was laughing. One of the guys was glancing around, ducking his head. The trees were tall and full and blue.

We came upon a grassy knoll, a swelling of the ground. Out of it a pipe rose up — a small, ornate metal chimney. People were lying around it, prone, arranged like sunbeams. We crept toward them. I could hear the people chanting as they put their faces to the metal. At first I couldn't make out the words. My body was filled with danger. We crept closer.

They were chanting, "Smell the dead. Smell the dead. Smell the dead. Smell the dead."

"There's a new body," whispered Turner. "You can sniff the gasses from the crypt."

"Smell the dead. Smell the dead."

I said, "That's what you brought me here for? To smell the dead?"

"Shhh!" said Turner. He looked momentarily flustered. He said, "It's a small town."

"Hey," said one of the guys in greeting. The people around the chimney looked up. I recognized several of them from my school. Some worked at Wendy's; most worked at Burger Queen. And Diana was there. I wanted to run. I stood awkwardly.

"Diana—" I said. I started to walk toward her. "How are you?" I asked.

She sat up. She turned her face away. "Oh, Anthony," she said. "Anthony, what are you—"

"It's those dorks from OD's," someone said.

"Hey," said one of the guys from BQ, a kid so cool his name was just Kid. "What brings you slithering around here, Turner? This is our turf, Turner."

"Came to introduce a new friend," said Turner. "His name's Anthony."

"He had a thing or two to say," said one of the guys who came with us. "He said he could whip your BQ butts."

"I did not—" I tried to say, but Turner stepped up beside me.

"He said he could!" Turner said. "He'll take you, man. He used to work at Au Bon Pain. He's special."

I was dying. Diana was looking at me, but I couldn't tell how. I couldn't see her face by moonlight. And Turner and his pals were yelling, "He says he can whup your stale little flame-broiled buns!"

I realized I'd been tricked, and started to back away, but already some of the BQ guys were getting up from the ground.

"You worked at the Pain?" one of them accused me, stalking closer. "You a goddamn pastry hawker?"

"I'm not," I said. "I'm not a pastry hawker. I never worked—"

Turner pushed me toward him. "Whup his ass, lily-boy." I tripped and stumbled.

Kid sneered, "You a goddamn limp-wristed beret-muffin? You sell croissants? Too good for burgers?"

"No," I repeated. "I really did not."

"Kid, my friend," said Turner. "I could beat you till your intestines were out and like all over, but I'm going to leave that to my boy Anthony."

This was starting to look like trouble.

I was pushed roughly from behind. I fell against Kid, pushing him backward. He shot out his hand and rapped me on the shoulder. He punched me in the gut.

"Stop!" cried Diana. "Stop it!"

I felt like I was going to puke. I fell to my knees. Kid thwacked the side of my head. I spun to the grass. I saw Turner jeering and starting to run backward. Turner yelled, "'Course I recognized you, you little shit." I didn't understand what he meant, at first. But he kept yelling,

"'Course I knew you in a second, sucker." And then it hit me that I was tricked, and he was saying, "'Course I knew you, bendy-boy. Good luck! Kick their asses and maybe the slut'll let you hold her hand."

He laughed hilariously and then he was bounding over gravestones while a few BQ bruisers chased after him. I couldn't follow. Kid was sitting on my back, slapping my head from one side to the other. I felt a huge rage. I reached up behind my back to grab him. He took my arm and twisted it. Diana was saying, "Stop it. Stop it. He didn't work at Au Bon Pain."

I said, "Ow! Ow! Ow! Ow! I didn't work at Au Bon Pain!"

"No?" said Kid. "No?"

"No!" I said through gritted teeth. "Never!"

Kid stood up.

Diana was standing over me. Her head was outlined against the stars. I could smell the earth. Some of the earth was up my nose. I said, "Diana. I love you."

"Shut up," she said angrily. "What are you doing hanging around with Turner? What the hell do you think you're doing?"

"Please, Diana," I said.

"You're so damn stupid," she said, and started walking away. The others were walking away, too. Some of them were giggling.

I crawled after her. "Diana?" I said. "Don't . . ." I made my way on all fours.

I sat against a gravestone for a second. They were gone. I breathed heavily. My stomach and cheeks still hurt. The stone was cool against my head. I spread my fingers out on the face of it.

I got up. I held myself up with one hand. I walked after them. I needed a ride.

They were gone when I got to the stone wall. All the cars had gone.

I remembered Turner's words: "Kick their asses and maybe the slut'll let you hold her hand." It made me angry. Very angry. I wanted to kill. I kicked the wall. It hurt my foot. I jumped up and down. I thought, *Okay, Turner. You got me this time. You got me, you bastard. But things won't go this way for long. This war is just beginning.*

The next day I was smoldering. I was buzzing with hate. My stomach was still a little sore. My legs were a little sore, too. I'd walked home five miles from the graveyard.

Jenn and Rick's shift overlapped with mine. They had heard about the whole thing. Jenn said, "I don't believe you went with him, Anthony."

Rick said, "It was kind of stupid."

Jenn said, "I guess you didn't know about that whole like rivalry between us and BQ. It's really, really big."

"Now I know," I said.

"They hate Turner," said Rick. "He's a marauder."

"He goes by his last name," I said.

"You would too," said Rick, "if your first name was Cyril."

"Ricky Licky and me spent the night watching videos," said Jenn. "Rick was doing this—"

Rick made some face. It was an impersonation, but I couldn't tell of what. He wiggled his fingers around his cheeks. He opened and closed his eyes. Jenn was in hysterics. She said, "Yeah, like that. Chug, chug, chug! Chug, chug, chug!"

Rick said, "Chug, chug, chug!"

I had no idea what they were doing. Jenn said between laughs, "Isn't he hilarious?"

Mike came around. Suddenly Rick and Jenn pretended to be busy loading the milk bag. Rick held the bag and Jenn steered the nipple. Mike took me aside. "Anthony," he said, "this is your first time on the lunch shift. It can be pretty crazy. Just keep thinking. Be aware. Calm yourself down. Clear your mind of everything but the Preparation Hierarchy: Drink, Sandwich, Fries. You can't go wrong if you just think of that."

I said, "Your years of training as a Zen master serve you well." I was irritable.

He said, "Anthony, I like a little sass in my employees, and can laugh right along with them. That's because I know we're all one big family. We're all in this together."

"I hear Kermit O'Dermott is coming here."

"Yes," said Mike. "They'll be shooting some footage at our franchise. It's something to be proud of. Now get out there and serve some customers."

I had never experienced anything like lunch rush. The lines were huge. People kept on ordering things. They just wouldn't stop. Some people were buying lunches for five or six people. To make it worse, Turner was my partner on register. Every few minutes, he'd come up behind me and say something mean.

"I'm Anthony, a little girl in a calico sweater."

Sweaters are not made out of calico, but that hurt nonetheless.

And the customers would be saying, "Yes, I'd like a . . . a . . . Big O Meal but with the Big O without tomatoes and extra salt with the fries, one small drink, a Coke I guess, and one large, a chocolate shake, no, not chocolate, one vanilla, a vanilla shake, to go please."

"I'd like a—what would you like, darling? A . . . ? What? Speak up so the man can hear you. She'd like a . . . say it, honey. Hamburger Happy Lunch. Annunciate your plosives. She wants a hamburger Happy Lunch. With a . . . speak up so the boy can hear. He looks new. Are you new? He's pressing all sorts of funny buttons, isn't he? He's talking to himself."

Turner, in passing: "Did you and Diana ever play shuffleboard? Did it ever get that wild?"

Rick calling to Jenn: "Genie Jennie Junebug? Would you get me a wee fry-o-rama-ding-dong?"

"Hi, yes, O'Chicken, fries, large, Coke, large, wait. Is that the meal? O'Chicken Meal. Or the Chicken Special. What's the difference? I'll try the Chicken Special I guess. That come with fries? I'll try that."

Turner, in passing: "Sir, you're being served by a wuss. Do you mind that? A complete wuss."

"Turner," I said. "You better—"

Jenn was singing to Rick, "When the moon hits your

eyes like a medium fries, that's *amore*."

Mike was yelling, "Would somebody put down more fries? Somebody?"

"Would you like that to go?" I asked.

"Sir, this kid is a real wuss. I'm not kidding."

"Turner!" I hit a few buttons. "That will be right up. Could I take the next order?"

"Two hamburger meal. Like the Two Cheeseburger Meal, but without the cheese. With Coke. That's one. Then a . . . can't read the writing. One sec."

"Four iced teas, please. Could I get them pronto?"

"Nuggets are up!"

"Ricky Licky—"

"Yes, Jennster Junebug?"

"Could you be snagging a nine-piece while you're back there?"

"I'm Anthony the bendable dork-boy. I'm not very strong, but I'm very stupid."

Beverage—Sandwich—Fries. Beverage—Sandwich—Fries. Beverage—Sandwich—Fries.

"Do you know the biggest reason I dropped Diana after we made out? Teeth. Just gross."

"Hi, I'd like the Big O hamburger sandwich for myself, with a soda pop and french fried potatoes. And for my daughter, a hamburger Happy Lunch."

"Okay, ma'am."

"Her teeth were not real."

A hideous beeping noise had started by the fries.

"And could you cut up my daughter's hamburger? Into small squares about yea big? She has trouble eating."

"I'm a bad, messy girl," said the little daughter. "I need to learn a lesson or two about neatness."

Mike screamed from the back, "Someone get the fries! Someone get the fries!"

"I can give you a plastic knife, ma'am. You can cut it up yourself then."

"No, could you just do that? Into squares about yea big. That's how big she likes them."

"Ms. Caroldi gave me three discipline tickets for lunchtime dripping and clutter."

"Pardon me. Pardon me. I had four iced teas and I'm afraid you'll find the bathroom is—"

Her teeth, Diana's teeth—how could he make fun of them? That bastard! The taste like the spice of the Orient, or dainty oysters. . . .

"Would someone get the fries?"

"Cut it up for my daughter and we'll wait here. Thank you."

"Get the fries, Anthony!" Mike yelled. "Anthony, go get the fries!"

"Ma'am, I can't—excuse me. I need to go get the fries. Be right back."

I ran to the fry machine. The baskets were down in the grease. It was bubbling furiously.

Turner was at my side. "Do you do ballet?"

"Turner," I said, "how do I get the fries out? How do I get the baskets up?"

The beeping was overpowering.

"See that big red metal ring by the side of the machine? Pull it."

He went and gave the lady and her daughter their burger. I walked carefully to the side of the fry vat and reached up to the red ring. I pulled it.

A shower of blue powder thumped out of the fume hood. It churned in the grease. An alarm went off. Mike came running over.

"Okay," I said. "I pulled the red ring. What do I do now?"

Mike said, "Oh damn." He told me what to do then.

We went out among the customers. The cut-up-hamburger woman and the dripping-and-clutter girl were sitting down to eat by the time I got to them. I waved. I said, "Hi, ma'am, there is a little problem and I'll have to ask you to put that hamburger down. The burger is now toxic."

"What? I bought it. I'm not going to put it down."

"Ma'am, this is a toxic burger. I apologize. Those fries are toxic fries. Everything in this store is toxic. I'm afraid we'll have to ask you to put them down."

She looked at her daughter. "Take your burger," she said. "Put it under your shirt and let's go."

"No, ma'am," I said. "The burger would still be toxic under her shirt. I apologize, but it is now coated with ammonium dihydrogen phosphate, a fire-retardant. We're going to have to close down for the day."

I could hear Turner laughing himself silly over by the registers. He was bellowing, "Store closed! Everything's poison! Poison orders only! Well done, Anthony my man! You are a genius!"

"Sir," I said to someone. "Please put down the coffee and leave the premises. I apologize. Because of me, your coffee is toxic coffee. Sir, because of me, that is toxic Sweet'n Low you're pouring into it."

So we got all the customers to leave. We locked the doors. All surfaces had to be cleaned. All the food had to be destroyed.

"Anthony," said Mike. "This was your first lunch rush. But you acted without thinking. Do you know what that was? Stupid. That was just plain stupid. I don't often call anyone an idiot, but look around you and see what we're going to spend the rest of the day doing. We will be working on our hands and knees. We will make no profit. In fact, we will make negative profit. I want you to think about that while you're wiping things down. Maybe you'll learn to ask questions the next time. Let me tell you an anecdote which may shed some light on the situation: My wife sometimes says to me, 'You're a complete idiot.' I take it as it's meant: constructive criticism. Okay?"

I considered telling him it was Turner. But I didn't think he'd believe me. And I thought this just added more fuel to the fire. I looked at Turner's sneer. He chuckled like a madman whenever he passed us.

Occasionally he'd say something. He'd stand next to me and polish. He would whisper things like, "Had to clean Margot like this last night. Really thorough. Takes a lot of Lysol to get wimp-stench off upholstery. Can't have the smell of wimp all stenching up my Olds."

So while I scrubbed and shined, I thought of ways to get even. One thing started to connect with another. I sprayed and wiped the metal surfaces. I thought about the things Turner would hate most in the world. I thought about how I could make them happen. I rubbed and scraped. I thought about hatred.

I thought about who could help me. At first, I thought of Rick. Rick felt sympathy for me. He would give me a hand. When I got together with Diana, he'd been pretty smug about the power of love. He was the obvious choice to help.

But then I looked over at him. He and Jenn were scrubbing with their sponge arms interwoven. They talked quietly to each other.

"You're the bestest at detoxifying."

"No, you are. You're the very bestest-beasty-estest."

Maybe not.

Dearly beloved brethren, we are here to mourn the passing of Richard Piccone's brain. Many of us remember Rick as an energetic, youthful boy with a strong interest in feats of endurance and the stupider of acrobatic stunts. Many of us recall with a smile Rick's enthusiasm for kung fu movies and his deep and reverent appreciation for airbrush portraits of barbarian warlords. We remember Rick the mountain hiker, Rick the devoted friend, Rick the concerned brother of a boy who won't get out of the bathtub. But no more. Rick was cut down in the flower of his youth, struck down by that scourge of manhood, that most repulsive of afflictions, called, in the medical community, lovey-dovey-cutesy-wa-wa. It ate through his brain like circus peanuts. Let us mourn him who is with us no more. Rick's brain is survived by his parents, his older brother, and his body. Please rise and sing the hymn.

Rick was out. That was fine. I would find someone else. I looked around the room. One of the cooks was an old stoner with stringy hair that was either brown, blond, or gray. I'd never met him. The woman working the window had kids. No help there. The other guy working register spent his free time selling his mother's prescription drugs to people working double shifts. He'd been fired from Burger Queen when he was caught trading amphetamines for chicken nuggets. He was easily angered and a biter. No help there either. I racked my brain. I washed and stewed. Then it hit me who. It all hit me at once.

Finally, I had a plan.

It was an elaborate plan. It was perhaps not the easiest plan to pull off. But it would be beautiful. It would be huge and ornate, like a torture machine. It would be inescapable, and would hurt poor Turner in many, many spots at once. It was the perfect plan for revenge.

So when I saw Shunt tying up the garbage and heading outside, I said, "Could I go out with you and see the trash compactor?"

And when we were alone there, I paused while the machine snapped and ground. Then I drew Shunt into conversation. He was saying, "You smell that smell? O'Dermott's garbage. A reek they try to hide. Distinctive. The secret rot of a multinational corporation. Ask: What I cook, how does it convert into this smell? The answer: mayonnaise in the Super Sauce. Going off. Like a sore they hide. Stink will out."

I said, "I hear you have an organization to undermine the fast-food chains."

He nodded. "I do. Burger Proletariat. You in?"

"I'm in," I said. "I have an idea."

"Oh?"

"For an operation. I know just where we can start."

"Okay."

"The first step involves a kidnapping."

"Hardcore."

"I can explain it all."

"Tell me," said Shunt.

So I did.

No one could hear us. The trash compactor banged and scraped. The scent of aging mayonnaise hung on the muggy summer air. Bees flew in and out of the palings of the fence. A few minutes later, we gave each other the high-five.

Then, agreed, we went back inside to scrub.

Chapter 3

. . . .

Some days seem perfect. By this, I guess I mean they seem like television. I thought a lot about the day when Diana and I went canoeing. When we stole apples together. Things had seemed perfect then.

The houses on the riverside had been well-painted. We could hear a lawn mower over the dribble of water from our paddles. As we went around a bend, we saw a house with pillars. A man was mowing the lawn with a beer-holder-hat on. A woman with her arm out stiff was crossing the grass in a negligee.

The apples rolled on the floor of the canoe. A spider was on one of them. When we rocked the boat and the apples clunked, the spider ran up the side of the hull.

Farther up the river, there were no houses. There were tall rushes. On either bank, there were just trees. Occasionally we saw a carton or a child's toy draped in dead weeds. The water stank like poison.

"Swamp gas," she said. "At night it lights up. They used to think it was the spirits of the dead."

We washed apples in the river and ate them. The river water on the skin added a delicate hint of muck and gasoline. The spider was back on the apples.

There was a slow and steady rhythm of dipping the oars. We went under bridges. They were concrete. Usually, there was graffiti underneath. Often it was years. *'76. '87. Class of '92.* Sometimes it was about romance. *K.L. + Anita, happy 4-eva. Rhonda, I love you. Cheryl, your for me, Bob,* corrected by someone to *Cheryl, you're for me.*

"I am like filled with awe," said Diana. "We're in the complete presence of history." Her voice echoed hugely.

"Yeah," I said, looking up at the years floating past in green and blue.

"Nineteen seventy-six. Can you imagine it? Dating in nineteen seventy-six? Graduating from high school and you think feathered hair will never go out of style."

"Where are they now?"

"I bet they have a flip."

It was like we were surrounded by the ghosts of fifties guys in cars with fins, sixties girls with long-dead flowers in their hair and orthodontic headgear. People now gone, now old, now working. I looked at Diana's back. The way stripes of light fell on it. Her arms were very real. Her hand cupped the head of the paddle. There she was, in solid flesh. Generations of American teenagerhood were telling me to seize the day before we became abbreviated numbers on the wall.

We came out into the light.

Cars rumbled on the bridge behind us.

Farther up the river, there was a factory that had been turned into offices. The river came out of a passage underneath the building where it used to turn a mill wheel. The river was very shallow. We could see the rocks and pebbles wobbling right under the canoe. The river moved faster here. We had to jam our paddles against the rocks so we wouldn't be swept backward.

"Should we go in?" I said. "There are probably weird chemicals."

"Sounds good to me," she said.

We forced our way up against the current.

It was tough going. The current was strong. We had to paddle hard. We kicked up a lot of spray. We knocked the paddles against rocks. I was afraid we would break them. They were my parents' paddles. I didn't want to say anything to her. There was no light inside the tunnel. The bottom of the boat scraped rock. It was aluminum, and squealed when it was scratched.

We dug our paddles into the riverbed and tried to crawl upstream. We couldn't see a thing. I couldn't see her. I assumed she was still sitting up there. I kept thinking about the metal things, the rusted things, that could be sticking out into the passage.

I looked behind us. The opening to the passage was just a small bright square. The noise of the river was big all around us. There was a stink of oil and rot. The canoe was too light. We were being shoved to the side. We were swiveling.

"I said," yelled Diana, "let's turn around!" She was standing right next to me.

"Sit down!" I said. "You're insane!"

With that, my paddle slipped, and the boat shot side-ways back down the tunnel. Diana lurched and fell onto me. The boat hit rocks with a clatter. The river was rushing all around us. The spray splashed us. I reached up and tangled my fingers in her hair. I wondered if she'd fallen on purpose. She was breathing on my neck. We were both laughing.

"Diana?" I said.

"Ow," she said. "Your knee is like right in my stomach."

We shot out into daylight.

I was sitting up carefully. I didn't want to bruise her or anything. She was crawling backward. A few people from the office building were dangling their legs over the river, eating bag lunches. Diana was straightening her shirt.

"I'm sorry," I said quickly. "I'm really sorry."

I grabbed my paddle and started to fix our course.

The river slowed.

She had dropped her paddle. It was floating off to the side. It had gotten caught on a fallen tree. I steered us toward it.

I hoped she admired my j-stroke.

I said I could maneuver us alongside it, but she wanted to wade. I brought us to the bank. She stepped out of the boat. She walked carefully. She wheeled her arms to keep her balance on the pebbles. I could tell they were cutting at her feet. I guessed her feet were soft.

She reached out for the paddle.

Her calves glittered in the sun.

It had only been a week later that she'd draped Turner's jacket around her shoulders and rolled on a couch while they were drunk. That day with the canoe seemed like a perfect day to me. I don't know whether it seemed perfect to her. Later I had to ask myself: The whole time, was I just a paddling fool? Or did she have as much fun as I did? She was laughing. That's proof. Laughing is fun.

I wondered what she was thinking as she lay on top of me in the dark. Did she expect something I didn't do? Was she disgusted, thinking I was taking the chance to grope her? Did she think I was this clumsy sicko, trying something on? Or did I seem too clean, too slow? I didn't know what she had thought. I didn't know what Turner had done to get her to do what he wanted. I didn't know what I had wanted that day on the river.

When you've spent a perfect day, how could it improve?

When I am feeling rotten, I like to walk. When you walk, there's a kind of rhythm. Your mind slows down to match your body. Your thoughts start to go in lazy, comfortable circles. I like to walk in the woods especially. Sometimes hiking through the forest you can see a doe or a hoot owl out by day.

I was walking through level B of the municipal car park. The halogen lamps buzzed. Moths nuzzled them. Big floppy-legged mosquitos were hanging on the walls. My footsteps echoed even down on level A.

There was a guard box on level A. Cars paid there. Level D was open to the air. You could get your ticket validated at one of our many excellent local businesses. You could park here up to a full day. The whole place was made of concrete and tar. I walked the height of it, all the way up to D, and down again. I had come to feel sorrow.

Diana and I had picnicked here together. We had spread the blanket on level C, near the wheelchair ramp. We had eaten egg salad sandwiches by candlelight. She had worn a red-checked shirt and ponytails to look like a girl advertising margarine. I had worn a strobing plaid. We curled our fingers together and read bumper stickers at eye level. We watched the senior citizens of the local euchre club file past like swans. We lay side-by-side, holding hands, humming the song "Memory" from *Cats* in unison until the exhaust got the better of us and we had to go retch on the roof.

Now I stood there, looking at the empty spot, C-24, where we had spread out our good basket of things. I thought about her. There were some jokes which she made and which I made that other people just wouldn't get. I thought about Turner. He really wouldn't get a Fume Picnic. I could see him thinking it was dumb and sissy. *What the—?!? Oh, cute. Real cute.* His head was made of meat.

I started my walk again. I picked up my pace, thinking about his head and its stupid, unfeeling, pockmarked steak. It was the kind of meat you wanted to hit. Your fist would make a nice smack. I couldn't see how he kept thoughts in meat. Only one at a time. One thought, wrapped in meat and strapped in with twine, like a roast. A chuckhead grinning above a jacket of green sateen.

Her kissing him. I saw it. She wanted to kiss that meaty face. That sneer. Sticking out his tongue. She had the tongue in her mouth like bad sirloin. She wanted that. I don't know why. I asked myself:

Why?

But I didn't know the answer. I was pacing faster and faster, up and down the spiral parking lot.

I was telling myself about my master plan. I was thinking about how it would be genius. It was so genius it was maybe even capitalized (Master Plan). I was thinking about every detail. The first stage—the kidnapping with Shunt—me, disguised ingeniously, providing the diversion while Shunt would do the deed. The second stage, waiting, sending letters through the U.S. mail. The third stage, the final revenge when Kermit O'Dermott came to town. Turner wouldn't know what hit him. No clue who'd pulled the stunt. Even Shunt wouldn't know the extent of the thing. If he knew it all was for revenge, he wouldn't help. He had to think my motive was hatred for the corporation. That way he'd help. I'd leave no spoor. This was the mastery of the Plan: Even Turner himself would never know it was me. No one could ever trace it all. I would make him cry.

I will make you cry. I thought about him getting pouty. I

thought about his chin wrinkling. His mean eyes blinking. And tears.

"I will make you cry!" I roared. My laughter echoed through the empty car park as if in a tomb. It echoed better when I tried nearer to the central air shaft. I experimented with some guffaws facing away from the air shaft. I moved about ten feet to the right and chortled. I took a few steps back. I cackled.

After some trial and error I decided that to sound really maniacal, I had to laugh at about knee level, five feet away from the central air shaft. That was fine, except that the evil rarely hunker.

I got on my knees. I stretched out my arms. I said, "Ha ha ha ha ha ha ha!" I cleared my throat. Sometimes I get this phlegm.

Then I had great peals of laughter. *"Ha ha ha ha ha ha ha! Yes, yes, Mr. Turner, I shall make you cry! Ha ha ha ha ha ha ha ha!"* Four frightened finches shot up the air shaft. *"I SHALL MAKE YOU CRY!"*

I could have used some lightning.

For hours before stage one, I worked on my disguise. It was impenetrable. I did not let my parents know what I was doing. I asked them if I could borrow the car. They said yes. When I had on my makeup and my special clothes, I sat patiently in my room. I sat on a chair in the middle of the floor. They walked from one end of the house to the other. They were calling to each other in different rooms. I waited until they were both in the kitchen.

Then I darted down the stairs and out the front door. "Bye Mom! Bye Dad!" I yelled.

"Have a good evening, honey!" I heard them call. "Say 'hi!' to Diana for us!"

I was not, of course, going to see Diana. That was just a clever ruse.

I ducked so the neighbors wouldn't notice me. In my costume, they wouldn't recognize me. They would think I was somebody stealing the car. My costume was very complete. When you are going to get some revenge, you must be a master of disguise.

I started up the car and backed it out of the driveway. It was still early evening. It wasn't yet completely dark. The sky was still strange colors over the Mastersons' jungle gym and TV dish.

I drove to pick up Shunt. I was hunched in my seat. I didn't want my wig to get static by brushing the ceiling. Small details are an important part of any sting operation.

I made my way toward the center of town. I slit my eyes and watched carefully. No one around me appeared to suspect anything. I was right on schedule.

Shunt lived in the bushes next to the QuickBank automated teller. I pulled up and honked the horn. He came out of the bushes, looking suspicious and professional. Something about him and his anger made me realize how protected I had been. He opened the door and slipped inside the car.

"Nice costume," he said.

"Thanks," I said.

He pulled the seat belt on with several sharp jerks. I looked around at the QuickBank kiosk. I said, "Shunt, ah . . . this really where you live?"

He nodded, evening reflecting on his shaved head. "Yup," he said.

Trying to be polite and conversational, I said, "Do you, um, have an account here or something?"

He gave me a funny look. "No. Parents kicked me out of the house. Couldn't stand the no hair and the being weird." He looked at his hands. He felt his knuckles.

"Man," I said, feeling sorry for him. "You okay out here?"

"Sure," he said. "Ma and Pa Butthole just slowed me down anyway. This a good place to crash."

"Great."

"It's convenient to a produce stand. There's a Port-a-Potty over there where I can take a dump. Hey, someone's old subscription to *Road & Track* comes monthly."

"I didn't mean to sound like you don't have a nice place here. Like that the bushes aren't nice or anything. They're really great bushes."

"Juniper," he said with some pride. "They're actually shaped professionally."

"Oh." I nodded. "Berries poisonous?"

"Yeah. Unfortunately. But no one promised me a rose garden."

"Man, Shunt . . ."

"That was a joke, pal. The rose garden." Shunt threw

both his arms backward over the seat. He strained and cracked his back. He grunted and pulled his arms back around. Then he said, "So what's the checklist for stuff to do before the operation?"

"We have an hour before strike time."

"We've got to cover the license plate."

"Right. I have some black construction paper in the back."

"Perfect. You're a real professional." I was proud he said that. Shunt had a hard streak that made you want him to take you seriously.

I said, "This is going to be easy as pie."

"Won't know what hit them."

"I'll provide the diversion while you grab the victim," I said.

He nodded. "This is going to be ace."

"We rule."

"High-five for solidarity." We gave each other a high-five.

He looked at me from head to foot. He was taking in the costume. He nodded with satisfaction. "Man," he said, shaking his head. "I admire your strength."

Strength. Now we were talking. *My strength.* I was excited about the operation. This was adventure. Here we were, lurking in a parking lot, about to drive off and do things illegal and tricky. This was Living. Just thinking of it, the way I'd make Turner cry when everything came together, I felt a grim strength bubbling inside me, felt like I should be throwing back my head and roaring with laughter to show the full brilliance of my Plan. No more wimp. No more wussy.

Shunt said with admiration, "It's not everyone who would dress up as a female clown for the cause."

I laughed and the bells on my collar tinkled. "Yes, it's a masterstroke, isn't it? It will be perfect for the diversion. I've been practicing my contortionist act. We are masterful. They don't know who they're dealing with."

He scratched his lower lip. "So why a *female* clown in particular?"

"Ah! Ah ha!" I said. I held up a finger. "Because there aren't too many contortionists in town. I don't want to be spotted."

"I've got to hand it to you. You go that extra mile."

"What about you? You were supposed to be wearing black pants."

"Oh," he said. "I have to get them. They're in my closet."

I squinted into the darkening bushes. "Where's your closet?" I asked.

He nodded his head over to the left. "Over in the Appledale development, five-sixteen Granny Smith Street. Can we swing by?"

"No prob," I said. I pulled out of the QuickBank parking lot.

It took us about ten minutes to get to Appledale. There was a big sign with a happy worm. I was saying, "I called ahead to the place to confirm our timing. I pretended to be someone invited."

"Genius, man. You're wasted on little gigs like this."

"Not at all," I said. "Not at all." I glowed.

We turned onto Granny Smith Street. I was excited,

nervous. I tapped the steering wheel in rhythm. Shunt picked up the beat and did some syncopations with his cheeks and breath.

We drove past his parents' house once slowly. There weren't any cars in the driveway.

"Go around the block," he said. "There's a culvert around back."

We drove to the back. We cased Golden Delicious Avenue. We could see the house through a few trees.

"Park here?" I said.

"Yeah. Turn your lights off."

We got out of the car and I locked it. It was dark now. We could hear a little stream running through the strip of woods behind the houses. We made our way down the back. I tripped several times. My shoes were big.

We hopped across the brook. No lights were on in the house. There was a little lawn with a dark wooden fence on either side.

Shunt and I made our way up the bank of the culvert and came out on the lawn. "Okay," said Shunt. "It'll just take me a minute to go in and get the pants. I'll be right out."

He crept toward his house, keeping close to the fence. He ducked low. His heavy black boots squished on the wet grass. A bug light popped and zapped. He had already made it most of the way to the house.

Suddenly, there was barking. A dark shape hurtled toward him.

"Shunt!" I hissed.

It was a dog—a mean-looking dog, a brown and

black dog. The kind of dog that looks like it has teeth that once they're shut don't come open. "Shunt!"

I only had time to call out his name twice. Then it was on top of him. Shunt toppled. I rushed forward. The dog was all over him.

Licking and hopping.

"Hey, Bakunin," said Shunt, knocking the dog on the side of the head. "How are you, boy? How's my widdle doggy-boy? How is dat widdle boy?" Shunt chucked the dog's chin. He ruffled its nape. "I miss you, boy."

He got to his feet and waved at me. The dog slammed its front legs into him. He whacked it. It grinned.

As it turned out, I had to give him a hand up to his window.

"You might want to take off those gloves," he said. "They'll get all dirty."

I took them off and rolled them up. I shoved them in my pocket. I lifted him up to the window. He jimmied it. With his palm, he knocked it back and forth. Finally it slid to the side. Bakunin was jumping on my legs.

"Down, Baku," Shunt hissed from above. "Down, boy."

"He's going to wreck my polka-dot dungarees."

"I said *down*." The dog stopped jumping. It looked confused. "You," he hissed, pointing at the dog, "are a damn good boy." The dog let its tongue fall out. Shunt grabbed the window frame. He heaved himself upward. His boot treads left red geometry on my palms.

He was inside. The dog stared at me. I pretended to ignore it. I fixed my grapefruit breasts. They had gotten skewed.

"Okay," said Shunt from up above. "I've changed into the black."

"You ready to come back down?" I said.

"One thing," he said. "Can I just brush my teeth? I haven't for like weeks. They're getting kind of mossy."

"Hurry up," I said. "We don't want to blow the operation."

"Excuse me," he said. "No anarchist needs to take lip from Bozella the Clownette." He disappeared back into the window.

A few minutes later, we were taping black construction paper over the license plate. At first, the tape wouldn't hold. Shunt used his shirt to smear the dirt and grease off. Then the tape stuck fine.

We pulled onto Golden Delicious and headed out of the development. We were going to Burger Queen.

BQ was on the edge of town. It was a place where several roads came together. We drove in that direction.

We were whipping through the suburbs. We passed the new strip mall. I was thinking about revenge. I was congratulating myself on taking action.

"You don't know how right it is to help the cause," said Shunt.

"Oh yes I do." He didn't know the half of it.

"These companies are monsters. You line up all the O'Dermott's hamburgers that have been sold? Circle the earth thirty-five and a half times."

"Wow," I said absently. I was thinking about the jacket of green sateen. And revenge.

"You don't know how their suppliers treat their animals. Pigs, chickens, cows: They live in pens too small for them to move. They're often conscious when they're slaughtered."

"Yeah, yeah, that's awful," I said, thinking about Turner and his vicious grin.

"Just one of O'Dermott's meat suppliers takes up to three hundred chicks a day that don't make the grade. Gasses them to death." He stared at me and said, "Carbon dioxide in a box."

"Those bastards," I said, making a left turn. I hoped he'd shut up. I could have used a minute of silence to focus.

On he blabbed. "All of them, they're all clear-cutting forests and jungles, kicking out native peoples."

"Are you sure?" I said. "They have a policy against that."

"Hello," he said, knocking on my head. "They're lying. It's a lie. It's been proven in court. They're buying meat from Costa Rica and Brazil. They're trying to change the eating habits of developing nations. They're producing one million tons of waste packaging a year, each chain. It's thrown away after approximately five minutes of use."

"Yeah, Shunt? Could we concentrate?"

"Meaning? You mean what?" He was a little angry. "This is concentrating. This is who we're up against."

I felt bad for tricking him. That's the way it had to be. "I'm sorry," I said. "Jitters."

"Don't freak."

"I'm not freaking. We're going to kick butt."

"Yeah," he said.

The Burger Queen was on a road with lots of gas stations. There were other chains, like Bruegger's and Dunkin' Donuts. All of them had bright lights against the night. There were figures walking through their parking lots. There were streaks of light on dark cars. Auto dealerships were empty.

We pulled into the Burger Queen parking lot. I parked the car near the entrance to the restaurant. I turned off the lights.

"Okay," I said. "You ready?"

"Ready," he said. He put up his sweatshirt hood. "Leave the keys for a quick getaway?"

I looked around. There were cars in the parking lot. No people. We'd be back in a minute. "Okay," I said. I moved my hand away from the ignition. The keys dangled.

I got out of the car. I stood for a minute, facing the restaurant. Shunt sat without moving. He wasn't looking at me. A blank stare was the only thing inside the hood.

I crossed the tarmac. I walked three steps along the sidewalk. I opened the door. I was faced by the promotional condiment troll. I walked right past it. I was in.

Earlier I had checked the big erasable calendar in the Burger Queen. They kept it on the wall near the registers. I'd written down when there were birthday parties. Today, I'd called to make sure the party was still on.

Sure enough, they were playing in a separate, glassedin space. About fifteen little six-year-olds. They were covered in grease and ketchup. There was wrapping paper all over the floor. There were little tennis shoe prints stamped everywhere on the paper. We wanted lots of kids there. Lots of kids would be the perfect diversion.

It was now or never. Do or die. And so the operation began.

I jumped into the glassed-in booth. I squeaked, "Greetings and salu-walu-tations, kiddikins! I'm Hippy-skippy, the wackster clown! The clown around town!"

They all stopped and stared at me.

A mother said, "We didn't order a clown."

I gave her a withering glance. "Well, you got one," I said.

There was a difficult moment.

Then I said, "Want to see me bend my bendable body into zaniful, insaniful shapes?"

The kids stared at me. They had round eyes, round mouths. I picked up my foot. I wobbled it back and forth. I grinned. I squirted some water from my flower. I put my leg behind my head. They put down their burgers and crayons. They came forward. They surrounded me.

I hopped on one leg. It was like they were hypnotized. I turned in circles. My big shoe was flopping next to my ear.

I sang in a high-pitched voice, "Do your ears hang low? Do they wiggle to and fro? Can you tie them in a knot? Can you tie them in a bow?"

I drew my sword. It wasn't a real sword. I laced it through my arm and leg, behind my neck. I sat down. I reached down and grabbed my other foot. I brought it backward. Sometimes this trick caused pain. I kicked myself in the forehead with my heel. I crossed my eyes, stuck out my tongue, and blinked like dazed. They didn't laugh. They watched me carefully. They didn't trust me.

"Don't try this at home!" I squeaked.

I brought the second leg over the top of my head. It knocked the wig. I stopped quickly. My leg was hurting. I fixed the wig. I brought the leg the rest of the way back. I hooked it next to the other one, behind my neck. I was a strange little package now.

"Wow," said a little girl.

"Cool," said a little boy.

"That's completely repulsive," said a woman.

A little boy came up to me. He had his finger pointing out. He took his finger, and he stuck it into my side.

"Ow!" I said.

They all watched me for a second. The little boy spoke in a voice as deep as a hoarse man's. He growled, "Poke the clown."

I guess this seemed reasonable to them. They all clustered around me. They started to poke me.

"Ow! Ow! Hey! Stop! No, this is—!"

"Poke the clown! Poke the goddamn clown!" the little boy croaked.

"Ow! Would you stop! Hippy-trippy doesn't like pokey-wokey!"

"I'm the birthday boy! I say poke the clown!"

"Poke it!" they laughed. "Poke the clown!"

They were all over me. They were jabbing me with their fists. The little girls were cackling. The boys were kicking.

"Okay! Okay! Stop! Hey! Ow!" I grabbed at my foot. I unlocked it from behind my neck. I tried to get up, but my other leg was still behind my head. The kids were pulverizing me. One kicked me in the face. My nose stung. One sat on my neck and leg. "You're going to bruise Hippy-hoppy! You're—would you lay off? You are insane! You are demon possessed! Is there a priest? I need a priest!"

The mothers stood to the side and discussed their children's Montessori schools.

I was completely paralyzed. My nose was starting to bleed. One of my breasts was on my shoulder; the other was on my hip.

A manager was heading my way. Half a minute and it would be too late.

I yanked at the leg behind my head. My fingers scraped over the big shoe. They locked around the tip of it. I could feel the grit on the sole. I pulled. The leg came free.

I rolled into a crouch. I stood, and moved backward. The brats were mobbing me. I could see Shunt in position, just outside the door, hanging back in the shadows.

The manager reached my side. I nodded once to Shunt and turned away from him.

"What's going on here?" said the manager.

"Okay, kids!" I screamed over the noise. "Time for a tour of the kitchen! Big prizes! Prizes! You get stuff! First one back to the flame broiler gets a free Billy Goats Gruff playset! Run!"

They were off. It was chaos. Little ugly sticky bodies were everywhere. People were yelling about danger and forbidden and grease fires. I was clapping and waving my arms. Shunt was in through the door, grabbing the promotional condiment troll, lifting it, shoving it toward the door.

The manager was running after the kids, grabbing their collars. The mothers were looking up.

I scampered to the door. Held it open for Shunt and troll. Took half of the troll. We were out of there. By the car. Back door open. Troll shoved in. People coming out of the restaurant. I pulled the handle for the front door.

"I locked it!" I said. "Damn, I locked it!"

Opened the back door. Unlocked the front door. Shunt sliding into his seat. An employee and a mother screaming threats. The mother running toward us.

I slammed on the gas. We lurched forward. The troll hit the seats. We screeched backward. Roared out of the parking lot. A truck honked, slammed on its brakes. We were off.

Cruising down the road. I pulled off the wig. With one hand, popped the snaps on the shirt. Pulled off the suspenders. Shunt handed me some paper towels. I handed him my breasts. I wiped at my face. I could feel the makeup smearing. He leaned over the back seat and covered the troll with a gray blanket. I gouged at my cheeks. My nose was still bleeding. The paint came off in cakes.

I raised my butt off the seat. I slid the big pants down. I had normal clothes underneath. I turned off the main road. We'd lose any pursuit.

We were safe. Shunt gave me the high-five. He peeled one of my breasts and gave me a few slices. They were tangy. We were laughing through the pulp.

We drove into the night.

Mission accomplished.

• • •

The condiment troll was four and a half feet in height. The surface was high-gloss. The skin was a watery green. The troll had knobs on his flesh, like acne or cysts. They were closer to brown. The troll's maw was gaping. Inside were straws. Most of the straws had fallen out of the maw in the getaway.

The troll had pointed ears. Pointed teeth, too. A pointed leather cap. In one arm, the condiment troll held a barrel of mustard packets. In the other arm, he held ketchup. The condiment troll was frozen that way. He had been made to offer spreads.

The expression on his face was hard to read. His smile was wide. Maybe it was supposed to make little kids feel better. Maybe it was wider than was natural. Maybe it was even a little hysterical. It was difficult to tell; he was a troll. His eyes were googly. Maybe that meant he was fun-loving. Maybe that meant madness. Maybe that meant he was hungry.

The condiment troll had been made to promote the new movie adaptation of "The Three Billy Goats Gruff." The story was basically the same as the fairy tale, with the three goats and the troll, except they added a goat-herd girl with a pencil waist and a big chest. In the mall, they were always playing the soundtrack. You could pass girls who had the album singing along near the potted trees. "I May Be Gruff, but It's Tough Love." "Can I Find Hope (Under a Bridge)?" When they sang along, they sounded both very old and very young at once. For the low notes, they dipped their heads and closed their eyes.

The troll was not singing. The paint on his knee had

been scraped. He was bowlegged. On the back of his left leg, in small raised letters, it said he was made in the Philippines.

His feet were bare. The condiment troll stood in an empty room. The floor was covered in linoleum. The linoleum was starting to peel and roll. The wood showing underneath was caked with dirt. Glass was on the floor in shards. Bees came in and went out. The day outside was bright.

The room that held the condiment troll was at the end of a long hallway. The hallway was dark. The floor was wood. It was uneven. Everything smelled like vinegar. Several places, the walls had been kicked in, and the plaster was crumbling. Maybe some kids had done it shouting, feeling drunk and mean. Maybe the last owner of the house had done it, as his wife ran screaming for the car.

Down the steps, there were rooms with no doors. One had some beer cans on the floor. The aluminum was fading. When it rained, the rain came in and tapped the cans.

Pine needles stuck to the floor of another room. Just against one wall. The glass was gone from the windows. Two of the rooms were black from flames. Fire had come up from the basement and covered the walls. People said something was buried in the basement. The floor was burned through. In the wind, these rooms creaked. They sounded like a ship at sea.

The front door was open. The woods were bright with sun. Squirrels ran by the stoop. Orange needles covered the path.

Three dark tracks led into the woods. Someone had kicked up the needles. There was dark loam underneath. These were the tracks where Shunt and I had dragged the troll. We had dragged him from the car at midnight.

The condiment troll stood in a room miles from anywhere. He stood upstairs, alone. Here he would wait until he was needed. He was a long way from anything. Sometimes he stood alone in light. Sometimes he stood alone in shadows.

By day, the bees sniffed his ketchup.

By night, the wind prowled through the empty house and rustled the straws in his smile.

Chapter 4

. . . .

You don't like it?" I asked.

"Wish it could be more political."

"You know it can't be political."

"Don't tell me what I know, Comrade Wiener. I'm just saying."

Shunt was in his street clothes. I was in my uniform. He leaned against the other side of the counter, reading my letter.

"It's very threatening," I said.

"I'm not complaining. Just, it's too bad we can't mention the proletariat."

"We stole a troll. Where does the proletariat come in?"

"It's all about the proletariat."

"It's about a condiment dispenser. Let me look at the letter again."

I read it through. For our purposes, it was perfect. It didn't reveal our identities. It said nothing about our motives. But it was threatening. It said:

TO Her ROyal
HighNess, the
mOSt MaJeStiC
aNd Regal
SOVerEign,
Empress Of the
FLame-BROiLeD,
PrOteCtor Of the
DOUbLE-DeCkeR
Jumbo,
The Burger QUEeN:

SO We haVE yOUr
troLL.
WOULdn't it be hard
tO disPeNSE
CONdimeNts With
NO ARMS?
NOW, WHO
deServes A breaK
TODAY?
With undying O'hatRed,
yOUr WOrsT
enemy.

"Like the font," said Shunt.

"Well, that's something."

"It's not often you find a font that can simulate hate mail."

"I'm bad with scissors."

"I don't mean to bitch. Given the circs, I think this'll be perfect."

"So you like it?"

"Sure. Looks fine, for subterfuge."

This was good. Shunt was an important ally. He had to believe that we were doing this all for a good cause. That we were trying to remain anonymous because we wanted the BQ franchise to think the whole O'Dermott's franchise was responsible for whatever went wrong. He wanted to raise the pitch of the battle between BQ and O'Dermott's, so they would destroy each other. Shunt had to believe that this was what I was interested in too.

It seemed to be working out. Except that Shunt was getting excited about parts of the plan that didn't mean much to me. "What I can't wait for," he said, "is for when the movement's spread and we can drop the anonymity. Let them have it. Point out the wage slavery. The enfeeblement of the American mind. The corruption of the corporate structure. The commodity fetishism of the marketplace."

"The fact their fries suck."

"You aren't like taking this seriously."

"Well, maybe I'd take it seriously if you talked like someone who'd gotten all the necessary tetanus shots."

"Oh, man. Oh, man!"

"Don't freak out."

He made a *pfffff! pfffff!* sound while he scrubbed his hands back across his blank scalp. He scrubbed two times. He mashed his palms against his eyes. Then he looked up. "Okay, dude, so I'm going to send this."

"Yeah. Send that, and then, as time goes on, we'll start to point out all the . . . that stuff. You know. Like the enfeeblement and fetishes and everything."

"All right. Out of here. I'm headed back to the shrubs."

"Man," I said. "How long are you going to live in the shrubs?"

"That's an indefinite arrangement. Hi, Turner," said Shunt, taking the letter from me.

I jumped. Turner was standing beside me.

"What're you boys doing?" said Turner.

"Writing you love sonnets," said Shunt. He blew Turner a kiss on his middle finger. With his other hand, he held the letter under the level of the counter. I was glad that he could be a very sneaky anarchist. He said to me, "Later." He left. The decals on the door flashed as he went out.

Turner leaned against the counter, grinning at me.

I stood. I tried not to stand like I was nervous. My weight was on one foot. I shifted to the other foot. As a foot, it seemed less nervous.

"That Shunt," said Turner. "He's a character."

I couldn't decide if it would be less nervous to have my arm up on the counter or just hanging. I tried it both ways. Turner didn't move. A customer came. I took her order. I was grateful I didn't have to look at Turner. He was still standing next to me. After I'd told the woman her total, I turned around to get a cup and start the drink flowing. Turner walked by my side. He said, "Question for you, Little Miss Wuss."

I shoveled some ice into the cup. "What is it, Turner?" I hit the button for medium Sprite.

"You play softball?"

"No."

"Come on, man. Everybody plays softball."

"I have, but I don't. What do you want?"

"Wait till you've got the fries."

"Okay," I said. I went and got her Big O, then the fries. I came back for the drink. Turner was fitting the lid. I hoped he hadn't spat into it or something. I went back to the counter. I gave her the food and the drink. She paid.

Turner said, "The softball game against Burger Queen. We need players bad. You're pretty fit. You could play."

"Thank you, ma'am. Six thirty-one is your change."

"Have a nice day," said Turner to her, smiling. He turned to me. The smile was gone. "What do you say?"

"No way, Turner."

"Look, man, I'm sorry about the graveyard. That what you want to hear? I'm sorry. It was completely bastardly of me. You're kind of a wuss, but I . . ." He shrugged. "Look, all I'm saying is, you went out in that graveyard last week and you stood up and took it like a man."

That was a funny way to describe crawling on all fours and groveling for mercy, but I wasn't going to argue. "Thanks," I said. "You have . . . well, like you have been kind of a jerk."

He nodded and shrugged. "I have. I am a jerk. I can't deny it. Yeah?" He gave me a playful shove. It almost dislocated my shoulder. He said, "That's what I am. Still, man. You took it. I'll lay off you for a while. Now what do you say to the team?"

"You're not captain, are you?"

"No. Mike is. He runs the whole show. He asked me to ask you."

"Is there a practice or something?"

"Sure," said Turner. "Saturday. Then next Saturday is the game."

"I'll think about it."

"You do that," he said, pointing to my head. He leaned next to my register. "I'll just stand here while you think."

I served a couple of people. Turner followed me around.

Finally I said, "Okay, I'll play. Now will you stop following me?"

"Customer," said Turner. His smile was suddenly huge and enthusiastic. "Hello, sir. How may we best serve your chowing needs?"

Once I agreed to play on the softball team, Turner made a gruesome effort to be nice to me. Maybe his team spirit was stronger than his bully instinct. In any case, he would lean up against the counter near my register and talk to me about his car, Margot, when he had free moments. He was much nicer, even though he still called me Little Miss Wuss. "I'm thinking about getting Margot vanity plates," he would say, or, "What are those reflecting things on the road called? You run over those things quick enough, man, I love them. They sound like the road has a heartbeat and it's only getting faster." And once, with no explanation, "You know it's a crime in this state to run over a cat and not tell the owner?"

Shunt and I were sitting at a table. We were on break.

Usually Shunt spent his breaks in back listening to the radio. He would hear about an explosion in Mexico or a company that fired a guy for getting an arm torn off in machinery. He would sit slumped in the staff room with his face in his hands. He would murmur, "My god. My god." Two forty-year-old men who worked grill would stand on either side of him, giggling silently and taping a "Kick me" sign to his back. Shunt took it hard.

One day we decided to go on break at the same time. Now that I worked mornings, our shifts only just overlapped. We both had fifteen minutes for break. We were sitting at a table. We were talking. Each employee was allowed five dollars worth of O'Dermott's food a day. I used mine on a Big O and fries for lunch. Shunt had gotten an Apple O'Pie slice. He was burning it. He fed pieces into a flame in an ashtray.

"Turner's trying to be nice to me," I said.

"Oh yeah?"

"He talks to me. The other day he was boasting about playing Cockney Roulette."

Shunt raised his eyebrows. A trail of greasy smoke rose between us.

"It's a night-driving game," I explained. "You turn off your headlights, talk in an English accent, and drive on the wrong side of the road."

Shunt nodded. "That's about the limit of European culture in this town." He fed his fire another hunk of pie. The syrup put the fire out. He said, "Ma and Pa Butthole are off in Europe right now."

"Who?"

"My folks. Jack 'n' Jill Suburb. The Middle-Management Twins. You know. They who spawned me one night when Johnny Carson was canceled."

I stared at his pie. It was a ruin. He still had half left to burn. The syrup had burned down to toxic candy.

I spun the ashtray slowly with a finger. Finally, I asked, "What's up with your parents?"

He didn't answer at first.

I said, "I mean, why . . . you know. Why you and the bushes?"

Suddenly he sang, "High-ho-ho, high-hee-hee. I hate them, and they hate me." He stood up and swept all the trash into his hand. He threw it away. "Lunch break's over," he said. "Last one to the vomitorium's a rotten egg."

"Shunt, I was just asking," I said.

"Well, I was just telling."

We went back to our stations. I only had another hour. I could hear Shunt in the back. One of the guys on grill had come in stoned, and was telling everyone knock-knock jokes. People back there were laughing at him. Shunt laughed loudest of all. He laughed like they were the funniest things he'd ever heard.

"Orange you glad I didn't say banana again" is just not that funny.

One day, I decided to test Turner to see how far his new nice went. I tried to start a whole conversation with him.

"So where . . . I mean, how did the whole friendly rivalry thing start with BQ?"

"It's not friendly. I hate their goddamn guts. I want to see them bleed."

"What did they do to you?"

"What? Why does someone have to do anything? I just hate them."

"It must have begun somewhere."

"They do stuff to us, we do stuff to them. Hate. It's that simple."

"But, I mean, how did the thing start?"

Turner shrugged. "I don't know."

"But when? I mean, it must go way back."

"I don't know."

"There must be like old stories. There must be lore."

"Lore? What's lore?"

"Stories."

"Stories? Hey!" he snapped. "Does this look like story hour? Do I look like an educational lamb-puppet?" He stared at me with a sneer. I could see each blackhead on his nose. He had acne scars around his chin and neck.

"No," I admitted. "You don't look like an educational lamb-puppet." I was cowering.

"I didn't think so," he said. "Now will you shut up? This is not a place for stories. There are no stories here. Free time? You should be wiping down surfaces. Goddamn, this team spirit thing, I'm trying to be nice to you, but it's difficult not to kick your ass." He swiveled on his heel. He rubbed his baseball cap. To the wall, he said, "You gonna replace the shake mix, or we gonna run dry?"

I backed away. I was heading for the cooler when Rick's brother came in. He was very tall and awkward. He slouched. He was wearing a brightly colored shirt, buttoned up to the top button.

"Excuse me," he whispered to me. "Is Rick Piccone here?"

"Hey, hi. It's me, Anthony. How are you?"

"I'm fine," he whispered. "It's nice to see you, Anthony."

"How are you doing? Rick told me you . . . weren't feeling good."

"I'm fine."

"Great, great, man," I said, patting him on the arm. "Rick was really worried about you."

He nodded his big head. "For a while, I wasn't well. I

thought everything was soot. That made me cry. I washed and washed myself. They took me to the hospital. I was medicated. Now I am hunky-dory."

"That's good to hear."

"I feel like a million dollars," he whispered, and grabbed onto my arm with both hands so hard the blood stopped.

"Uh, hey, why don't I just go back and get Rick?"

He let go. He smiled. "I am running some errands. I can do things for my mother and help around the house."

"I'll send Rick up."

I went to the back. Rick and Jenn were cleaning trays. They were getting hyper with the spray nozzle.

"Who knows where Serpico the Serpent will strike next?" said Rick. "Vvvvat! Vvvvvvat!"

"Oh, Rick! Rick! Ricky Blicky, don't! Don't!"

"Rick," I said, "your brother is up front."

"Rick, did you hear that? Put down the nozzle!"

"Abrupt wet T-shirt contest!"

"Thanks, Rick," I said. I wrung out my tunic.

"I think Anthony wins the wet T-shirt contest," said Rick.

"Rick," I said, "your brother's up front. Polyester doesn't melt in water, does it?"

"Catch you two drones later." Rick left.

Jenn and I were left alone. Both of us were kind of wet. Jenn was laughing. She shut off the water in the stainless steel sink. When the water stopped, the spigot creaked.

"He is so funny," she said.

"Yeah," I said. "He's a riot."

She creased her brow. "What do you mean by that?"

"I don't know. I haven't seen him much since you two started mashing up against each other."

She looked up at me. She looked a little concerned. "You're kind of feeling like a third wheel."

I shrugged. "Naw," I said. "I don't even feel like I'm close to the bicycle."

"It's not that we don't think about you. We mean to call. I'm really sorry."

"That's fine. I spend my free time walking in the municipal car park and hatching evil schemes."

She laughed a little. "You're still the same old Anthony."

"No," I said. "I don't think I am."

She looked down at the tile floor for a minute. Then she looked up. "You're still pretty cut up about the Diana-meister, aren't you?"

"I'm pretty cut up about that."

Jenn patted me on the arm. "I'm sorry, Anthony. We're still your friends." She leaned back against the sink. She shook her head. "I'm sorry. It can't be easy to watch people as in love as the Rick-bear and me are when you're feeling so alone."

"Don't worry about it. I've hardly seen you, except at work."

"I mean, because we're so cuddly and happy."

"And because when you kiss it sounds like someone stirring Jell-O?"

She said earnestly, "You and Rick should go have a boys' day out. You could go hiking or something. You could talk boy stuff."

I waited for a minute. I asked softly, "Do you ever talk to Diana?" Jenn didn't answer immediately. She put her hands behind her on the rim of the sink. "Yeah," she said. "Not as much as I used to. I thought she was pretty mean to you. Do you talk to her?"

"No. I don't want to call and bother her."

"Do you think it would be bothering?"

"I don't want to be a stalker."

"Anthony," said Jenn, "nobody thinks you're a stalker. I know how it is, when you don't want to seem pathetic."

"That's how it is right now."

"You're not pathetic, Anthony. She really screwed you over."

"What does she . . . you don't have to tell me, but does she say anything about me?"

Jenn thought about it for a minute. Then she nodded. "She's talked about you a couple of times." She kept on nodding.

I nodded back.

Finally, I said, "Okay. What did she say? Can you tell me?"

"She said she was really sorry. I think she is. She said she—"

"Anthony!" said Mike, walking around the fryer. "Explanation as to why you are not at the register? Explanation about the shake mix? Which you were supposed to get? Hello, hello, Anthony!"

"Oh, man, Mike. I'm sorry. I'll go right now and—"

"No, Anthony. Turner will send Rick to get the shake mix. Rick will work a register. You're going to have a little talk with me."

"Oh."

"We're going to have a little talk about team spirit. Would you come into the office?"

I went into the office.

"Anthony," said Mike, "I'd ask you to take a seat, but this is a five by seven cubicle with only one chair." Mike thought for a minute. He felt his mustache with his finger. He stopped feeling his mustache. "Anthony, we have a problem. We have a problem, don't we?"

"No. No, sir."

"Yes, Anthony. A problem is exactly what we are having. Let's look at you for a second, Anthony. Let's look at the person you are. You're a person who can't be relied on, because you won't go back and get the shake mix. Instead of that mix, you start flirting."

"I wasn't flirt—"

"Tsh!" he hissed, holding his finger up to his lips. "Tsh! You're a person whose uniform is wet. Who wants to see a wet uniform? People will think, 'Look at that boy. I bet he wets the nuggets.' You're a person—here, look here—you're the person who—look at this past week in the log book. Look at it, Anthony. We're talking shortages. Major, major shortages in your drawer. Fifteen to twenty dollars almost every day. A few more days like this, and we're going to have to let you go. Are you bad at math? I mean, really, really bad? Or are you stealing? That's something we have to establish."

I felt sick to my stomach. "Mike," I said, "I'm pretty good at math. I don't understand. I'm pretty good at it." I put my hand on my stomach.

"Think, Anthony. Maybe thinking will clarify the problem. For example: I can't say I'm good at everything. I can't ride a horse. I can't shoot a rocket to the moon. We can't be good at everything, Anthony, that's what I'm saying. So think about it. Go home at the end of your shift today. Go upstairs to your room. Look in the mirror. Ask yourself: 'Am I really, really bad at math?' If the answer is yes, we'd better do something about it."

"How did you know my room is upstairs?"

"See? You're the kind of person who develops paranoia. Anthony, everyone's room is upstairs."

"Look, I don't understand what's happening."

"That's exactly the kind of lack of awareness I'm criticizing. You are not someone who takes stock of your surroundings. But you have to take stock. Taking stock is what it means to be part of a team. Part of a family. Part, specifically, of Team O'Dermott's. Okay? Got it, Anthony? I don't mean to be harsh. But I like to run a tight ship. I like everything to be spick-and-span. Clean as a whistle. Is that understood?"

"Yes," I said.

"No: Is it understood?"

"It's really understood, Mike. I'm really sorry about the shortages. I honestly don't know where they've—"

"I'm sure you don't, Anthony. But that's not good enough. I'm going to be revising your schedule. You're going to be coming in for the early morning shift. You'll hear about it. Now go out there and move some product."

I went out to the counters. A bus of senior citizens had just arrived. They kept Rick, Turner, and me busy for a while. We got them all coffees. A lot of them wanted fries or hamburgers, too. The whole time, I was thinking about how much I was screwing up. I felt like I was going crazy. All I wanted was Diana. Somehow I thought if I were kissing her again, and telling jokes, everything would be all right. I pictured us watching some comedy, some zany comedy, with our arms around each other on the sofa.

"Hey," said Rick, shaking my arm. "You zoned."

"Sorry," I said. Now I was screwing up because I was standing around thinking about screwing up. There was no time to think. I struggled to get the lid on a coffee. The coffee spilled down the sides. It browned the gutter. It stung my fingers. I took a napkin and daubed the cup. I took the cup to the register. I counted the change exactly. I didn't make any mistakes.

The next person wanted a Big O Meal. After that, a hamburger Happy Lunch. After that, a cheeseburger. After that, a Big O Meal, a Chicken Special Meal, and a medium fries. After that, four iced teas.

The lines went back, and back, and back. More people kept coming in. Young and old. They yelled to each other. They gave each other the high-five. They cried in highchairs. They argued about directions. They didn't know what they wanted. Some of them were in families. Some of them were alone. The lines kept growing. I ran for the drinks. I got them fries.

They waved their arms. They tapped their fingers. Their mouths were always open.

Early in the morning. Turner and me leaning on the counter; both of us staring out at the fog. A kid I didn't know working grill, singing, "Michael, row the boat ashore. Allelujah." Outside O'Dermott's, no motion, just gray. A few truckers had come and gone. That was all.

"So tell me," said Turner.

"Mm-hm?"

He asked, "Distance equals rate times time, yeah?"

We could see our faces reflected in the glass.

"Yeah," I said.

Turner shifted his elbows on the counter. The unsteady voice came from the back: "Sister, trim the flapping sail. Allelujah." Through the fog, we could see the outline of a tree. The play area was almost invisible.

"My, uh, grandfather was from around here," said Turner.

"Oh yeah?"

"Farthest he ever went was, I don't know, Boston."

I picked up a cloth and wiped down my register. Turner kept staring out the window. He was whispering to himself and pointing at the air. I stuffed the rag back in the space between the counter and the register.

"So this trucker comes in and orders like two hash browns," said Turner, in a voice of awe. "Gets back on the interstate and takes off at like what, sixty-five miles an hour? Eats the hash browns. Shits 'em out what, like six hours later?"

"Eh. Our hash browns are pretty lubricated."

"Five hours, okay, five hours. Some truck stop, guy shits 'em out. Distance equals rate times time. That puts him layin' the cable three hundred and twenty-five miles away. Somewhere across the state border. See what I mean?"

I thought about it for a minute. "No," I said.

With something like a gentle sadness, Turner said, "Man, what I'm saying is the hash browns I serve go farther than my grandpa ever did."

Rain had been falling for two days. The woods were wet. They smelled like moss. The green was deep and dark.

In the ruined house, there were many leaks. Water tapped on the old, faded beer cans. It sounded like someone creeping up the stairs. Strange stains were spreading in the rumpus room.

I couldn't do it. I had the hacksaw in my hand, but it was resting on the floor. I slumped against the wall, one leg out straight in front of me. I stared at the condiment troll. The condiment troll was smiling. It was hopeless. I couldn't do it.

I was supposed to saw off a finger or horn. Then I was supposed to send it to Burger Queen. That would make them sit up and notice.

I looked up at his big, goofy face. He was looming over me. He looked a little menacing. He looked pathetic. I couldn't do that to something in human form. There was just no way.

"You are fiberglass," I said. "You're just a shape made out of fiberglass. You could be in a different shape." I tried to think of the condiment troll as being just a condiment stand, not shaped like a person or any particular mythical being.

But he was smiling at me. I tapped the tip of the hacksaw three times against the floor. The rain pattered out in the woods. It fell through the leaves.

There was no way I could cut the troll. I could almost hear him scream.

Fiberglass, I told myself. *Fiberglass!*

It didn't do any good. He had wide eyes. If you were sawing him, they would look wide with pain.

I no longer wanted to get revenge. I was falling apart. For a while, I'd been enjoying myself playing the evil avenger. I guess I'd enjoyed it too much. So much, I'd stopped feeling angry. It all seemed like a joke, now. Especially since Turner had turned down his jerk volume.

It wasn't even funny anymore. That's what I realized. I was getting bored with it. I didn't feel as angry, and it was no good pretending I did. I just felt depressed about the whole thing. I sat in the ruined house, and felt depressed.

I have got to get a grip on myself, I thought. *There has got to be more time spent doing my job right, less time spent mutilating trolls.*

Sitting in a ruined house with a hacksaw suddenly didn't seem very entertaining. It didn't seem like a good way to get things done.

I decided to abandon the Plan for the moment. Take a few days off from being an insane genius. Calm myself down. See what I really wanted to do.

I braced myself against the wall and stood up. The troll was already standing. "Okay," I said. "You're off the hook." I patted him on the head. "Fiberglass," I muttered.

I tromped down the hall. I left the troll behind me. I turned back to look at him. I still couldn't tell whether he was happy, hungry, or hysterical. I went down the stairs. They shook with my weight.

Outside, the air smelled musty. It was a little chilly. The rain had picked up again. I tried to cover my father's hacksaw with my sweater to stop rust. I think rust can creep when you least expect it. I walked back along the path. Thunder started in the distance. Warm summer thunder. Water dripped off branches. Leaves that brushed my face were cool, and licked my forehead. My clothes stuck to me. The rain had made them wet. Somehow, it felt like the bath I needed.

No more Mr. Nasty, I thought. *That's it. I'm through.* Having said that, having made that decision, I felt a sudden lightness. I laughed out loud. I almost did a dance. I half-spun. I threw my arms out wide. I ran into a birch.

It shivered and dropped water. *Fine,* I thought. I shook myself. I was soaked.

"Whoops, that one got you!" said a man's voice. I looked up. There were a young man and a young woman in rain slickers, going for a walk in the forest arm-in-arm. We all laughed.

"You're soaked!" she said.

"Yup." I grinned. "I sure am." My hair was plastered to my head. I started to dry the hacksaw with the sweater. "Even my hacksaw!" I rubbed it vigorously. Lightning cracked above me. I looked up. They were looking at me funny and moving backward. "Oh," I said, pointing toward the hacksaw. They started running. "This?" I said. They were running even faster.

I ran after them, trying to explain. "No, this is just . . . hey, wait up!" They ran faster than me. After a while, I was just enjoying leaping over branches and shrubs. My clothes clung to my body, and the air blew through them. I felt naked and free. When I got back to my parents' car, I was laughing, but shivering with cold.

On the way home, I listened to pop on WBST, the Boost. The rain on the roof sounded happy to be there.

One day that week, while I was watching the tropical fish on television, she called.

"Anthony?" said my mother. "Diana's on the phone."

"Okay," I said. I was suddenly nervous. There was a lot riding on every conversation with her.

My mother came in with the phone, talking and smiling. "So how have you been?" she asked Diana.

Diana answered.

My mother said, "I know, we haven't seen you for ages. Now don't be a stranger!"

Diana answered.

"Okay, here's Anthony. I know he's been dying to talk to you. Bye!"

She handed me the phone. She leaned on the door frame, smiling and watching me. I was trapped. Try to go to my room and I'd hear nothing but static. I put the phone to my ear.

"Hello," I said.

"Hi, Anthony."

There was a long awkward pause. On the television, a voice coming out of a big weed said, "The tautog darts for its mollusk prey, but cannot dislodge it. The tautog will have to feast elsewhere today."

"Let me turn down the volume," I said. I picked up the remote control. I muted the television.

There was another long awkward pause. Now there was nothing to hide the silence.

Finally, Diana said, "How are you doing?"

I looked at my mother. "Great!" I said.

"Look, Anthony: I just talked to Jenn. She told me you aren't 'great.' I am really sorry about all this."

My father's voice came from the other room. "Invite her to dinner for tomorrow night. She can have chops, too!"

"Yes!" my mother whispered. "Dinner!"

I didn't know what to say, with everyone watching me

and listening to me. I tried, "I'm watching a show about tropical fish."

"Anthony, I was serious. It's important to me that we really do be friends."

"Yes," I said warmly. "To me, too."

"But when I say 'friends,' I mean only friends. I really apologize for that night with Turner. That was really stupid of me. *Really* stupid. But at the same time, it like showed me a lot of things."

I asked, "What were the things?"

"I can't talk about the things right now."

"If it's just Turner, I forgive you in like a minute. A split second." My mother heard my tone. She heard the word *forgive*. She was starting to get a concerned look on her face.

"Has he asked her to dinner yet?" called my father.

I asked, "Was it the Turner thing?"

"It's not the Turner thing. That Turner thing was just a symptom of the other things. Do we have to talk about this right now?"

"I need to understand."

"Are you really trying to understand?"

"I need you to tell me."

"Anthony, it's just—look, I don't know how to say this. It's just—"

Mrs. Gravitz from next door said, "I cannot remain silent any longer. Little miss, you should be ashamed of yourself. Can't you see you are breaking this boy's heart?"

"Hello?" said Diana.

"He is a sweet boy. I'm telling you, young lady, you

are not going to find a sweeter boy anywhere else soon, especially nowadays, when all the young men are hooligans who hunt the streets, stealing appliances and breaking into computers and calling each other 'blood pal.'"

"Ask her to come over for chops!" my father said. "Afterward, we'll have a little Ping-Pong tourney!"

"Hi, Mrs. Gravitz," I said.

"Mrs. Gravitz?! Tell her to get off the line!" said my mother. "You're having a private conversation."

"What are they yelling about in the background?" said Diana. "Your parents."

"They're inviting you to dinner tomorrow."

My mother nodded proudly.

"This isn't going to work," said Diana.

"Why not?"

"Can't she come?" said my mother.

"Listen, young lady," said Mrs. Gravitz. "This boy is an angel. He is a saint. He should be declared a saint by the pope in Rome."

"You haven't told your parents yet, have you?" said Diana.

"No," I answered. "Not quite yet."

"Anthony!" she sighed. "You've got to deal with this! It's real. I'm sorry, but it's real."

"You can understand . . . ," I said miserably.

"There's nothing to understand, Anthony," said Mrs. Gravitz. "Was this girl unfaithful to you? Is that what it is? Don't get yourself mixed up with one of these little tarts."

"Mrs. Gravitz," I said. "Please get off the phone. I can't hear myself think."

"Mom," said Mrs. Gravitz's daughter, somewhere on the other line, "you really should let them talk. Anthony, maybe this girl would be more receptive if you backed off and gave her a little me-space. Have you considered that your affection might be crowding her?"

"Diana," I shouted through the hail of voices. "Diana, I really just need to talk to you."

Diana said, "I'm not sure what good talking would do. This is too crazy."

"It's not crazy, Diana," I pleaded. "It's only crazy because the portable phone is screwed up."

"I just can't deal with this."

"Diana . . ."

"This was a mistake to call you."

"No it wasn't."

"I've got to go." I heard her hang up.

Finally, there was silence on the line. My mother was watching me.

"Okay," I said to the empty phone line. "If not tomorrow, then maybe sometime next week. All right. Great. Good-bye, then."

"Anthony," said Mrs. Gravitz. "The little trollop already hung up on you."

"Thank you, Mrs. Gravitz," I said. "Thank you so much."

I pressed the off button on the phone.

"Not coming?" said my mother.

"No," I said.

"Nothing wrong, is there?"

"No," I lied.

I turned off the TV, and went outside to walk.

．．．

We had one softball practice before our game against Burger Queen. It was on a muggy day. We did some warm-up exercises first. We ran around the field a few times. I ran well.

My batting, on the other hand, was not great. I am not very coordinated. Later I kind of screwed up in the outfield. It was hot and my shirt felt wet and sticky. I stopped concentrating.

I don't like really like team sports. I can't stand all the stupid things you have to shout. I don't like being required to get loud and excited. I don't understand why some people are so anxious to prove that they are better than other people. Especially at games that only show you're better at skills I'm not sure are needed very often, like:

— hitting a piece of skin with a stick
— running so you can touch rubber
— grabbing dead things that fall out of the sky.

I stood there in the outfield, trying to think of other scenarios where those particular talents come in handy.

I hadn't come up with a single one when the ball landed beside me. People swore at me and told me to stop dreaming. I felt a little sheepish. The batter made it to third.

In general, though, I guess I wasn't bad. I wasn't the

worst on the team, in any case. This guy named Stan had burned himself with the fry rack the week before and he couldn't even put on his glove without going "Woooeeeoooeeeooo." He took off his glove and shook his hand out. On the back of his wrist, there was a criss-cross of red welts. When he finally got the glove on and caught a ball, he fell down, and started shrieking lots of things including blasphemy and the names of the whole urinary tract, from the bladder down.

When Mike saw me run, I think he was a little more pleased that I was on Team O'Dermott's. It was the one time he talked to me all day. Even Turner was impressed. The next day at work, he came up to me and said, "You aren't good at softball. But hey: You don't suck."

I was not always proud to be wearing the O'Dermott's green. When you are wearing a green polyester smock, people don't treat you like another person. Fathers talk to you like you're a machine. Mothers talk to you like you're slow and inbred. Kids talk to you like you're sad. Usually they seem rich. It seems like they're going to spend the summer's day doing something sunny, exciting, and warm. Sometimes they have their own cars. Sometimes their cars are expensive. They seem like they're going to the beach, or to someone's house. They don't mind showing off their skin to each other. They talk to each other in the line, even if they don't know each other. They didn't talk to us, the employees, unless they knew us.

This is probably unfair of me to say. A lot of them probably had jobs at garages or convenience stores. But somehow they didn't act like it when they came in for lunch or dinner. They acted like they were out on the town.

It was hard not to feel ugly. Crusty. Doped. My fingernails were black. My shirt was stiff. My hair hung flat. My skin was shellacked with ambient lard. I had to move as quickly as possible to keep the line down.

When two girls came in wearing half-shirts, their skin looking fresh, their hair full and glossy, their shorts clean and tight, it was hard not to feel like a dork. Their flesh looked more refined than the flesh I was serving them. Maybe they noticed me looking. They looked at each other. I shied away and stared at the register. I said, "Welcome to O'Dermott's. May I take your order?"

"Are we sure what we want?"

"We're not sure what we want. Do you have any recommendations?"

"I think you'll enjoy numbers one through six."

One said, "And the house specialty?" She raised an eyebrow.

I pursed my lips and suggested, "Number four tastes different going in from when it comes out."

"You," one of them said, smiling and almost touching my nose with her finger, "have a bad attitude."

"I don't mean for my attitude to be bad. I'm under a great deal of pressure at my dynamic and high-paying job."

"While outside it's a nice day."

Something about them made me feel bold. I nodded. "Now you get the picture. My shirt and pants are made of polyester. I ate a number two for lunch. My badge spells my name without the *h*. Can I ask: Are you ladies going out on the town?"

"Oh, yeah. We're painting the town red."

"I thought so. Are you leading glamorous lives?"

Now they were flirting. I was liking them more. They were looking at each other and giggling.

"We're going to the opera."

"We're off to the Ice Capades."

"Does your chauffeur have a gun and Grey Poupon?"

This, I thought to myself, *must be the way that people are charming. Then you find a clever way of seeing if you can meet them later. Then you arrange something. Then you all go out, and get to know them, and you have a good time, and before you know it, you are leading a normal teenage dating life, instead of one where you squat in an abandoned house, cooking up ways to cripple trolls.*

They ordered and I took out a tray and put a tray liner on it. I went to get the food. I hit the Sprite button and started filling the cup. Turner was at my side. He said, "Shit, man. Two babes! Babe-o-licious!"

"Yeah," I said curtly, and yelled, "Grill!" back to Shunt. "Double ham, no onions."

"You scoring?" said Turner.

"I'm serving their food."

"You can score and serve, man."

"Yeah," I said, and headed off for some nuggets.

Turner was talking to them when I got back to the tray.

"You are being served by O'Dermott's finest, ladies," he said. He grabbed my shoulders. "Allow me to do the introduction thing. Anthony. This is Anthony."

"Hi," I said. "Your double hamburger will be a minute." I told them the total.

"Nice to meet you," one said.

"Anthony is a fine young man," said Turner.

I nodded. "I'm the talk of the town," I said. They laughed. They probably thought Turner and I were wacky friends.

"It's nice to meet both of you," said one of the girls.

"Would you like sauce with those nuggets?" I asked.

"Anthony is a nice boy," Turner said. "That's what you need to know about Anthony. He's a nice, nice, nice boy. Aren't you, Anthony?"

"Okay, Turner. Thank you."

"Anthony is a little angel. Anthony is a complete sweetie-pie."

"Thank you, Turner. You can stop now."

"Anthony is a real man. That's what I like about Anthony."

"A real man. Thank you, Turner."

"Other men, when they found me on top of their girl-friends, half undressed? They might've cried. But not Anthony. No, there I was, on top of his girlfriend, with my tongue about halfway down her throat, but did Anthony cry? No. He was too much the man. You're the man, man! You, man, are the man!"

"Turner!"

The two girls were looking nervous. They were look-
ing embarrassed. There were several people in line
behind them now.

"No!" Turner cried, speaking now to the whole
counter. "There I was, half undressed on top of Diana
Gritt, the girl of his dreams. But did he cry? There I
was, feeling her tits. *But he did not cry!* No way! No damn
way! He ran! He saw who he was up against, turned
around, and ran! Anthony ran away! Because he is a
good boy! A nice boy! That, my friends, is a very, very,
very nice boy!"

"Could I have my change?" asked one girl, holding
out her hand. "Is our food ready?"

I looked down at the drawer. Turner's hand
shot back.

It was then that I saw it. I saw the obvious: Turner
had taken a ten and was holding it under the edge of
the counter, behind his back.

"Turner!" I said. I slammed the drawer shut. "You
took a ten!"

"I didn't take a ten."

"It's in your hand!"

"Try to grab it. If you can grab it, you can have
it back."

"Um, I'm sorry," said the girl. "I still didn't get
my change."

"Grill's up!" yelled Shunt. "Come and get it! Swallow
hard before the fat congeals!"

I was so ashamed, I turned my back on them all. The
girls were looking at me like they were deeply sorry.

Everyone in the line was looking at me. I put together the girls' order. I took the special order from the top of the bin. I felt so embarrassed, I was weak. I felt like I needed to sit down. I needed to kick something. I needed to break something. I went back to the tray. I put the sandwich down on the tray. The girls weren't even looking at me anymore. Turner wasn't around. I guessed he was getting rid of the ten.

I slid the tray toward the two girls. "Have a nice day," I said.

"You didn't give me change."

"I'm sorry," I said. "I'm really sorry. He—" I didn't get any further. I gestured back where Turner might be. I felt myself blush. My face was stinging. I released the drawer. I took out the change. I counted it carefully.

"Actually," said one of the girls, "maybe we could have this to go?"

I took out a bag. I put my hand inside the bag and flattened out the bottom. I put it on the counter. I took each item off the tray and nestled it carefully in the bag. People in the line were getting impatient. They were tapping their feet. Rattling their keys. I double-folded the bag. I pushed it toward them.

"Have a nice day," I said.

In my next free moment, I stormed back and knocked as loud as I could on Mike's door. He had been in back during the whole thing.

He opened the door. "What's the problem? You are knocking very loud."

"Mike—"

"I'm not deaf. You could knock quieter."

"It's Turner. I was just out there, and he started talking to these girls I was serving, and I looked down, and he was stealing money out of my drawer."

"Whoa, whoa, whoa. You're saying Turner was illegally removing fundage without change or recompense? Unbalancing the drawer?"

"Yes."

"Deliberately?"

"Yeah! I just saw him! I've been wondering why he's being so nice to me, always coming over and talking to me. He's been taking money the whole time."

"You say it's been him, standing there, taking money out of your drawer."

"I like wondered what was going on. It was him the whole time."

"Could you come in here? Come in the office."

"Okay," I said. "Sure, Mike." We went in. He closed the door behind me. Behind him, Turner came along, saw us through the window, and waved cheerfully.

"Listen here, Anthony. Listen up and listen good. You better be serious about this."

"I'm completely serious. He has a personal thing against me. He's been trying to get me fired from the start."

"That is ridiculous. Turner is one of the most faithful and long-standing members of our O'Dermott's family. Turner is sometimes not very nice, but he wouldn't do something like this. Turner has been the Cashier of the Month four times."

"I am telling you, it wasn't me! It was him! That day when I pulled the fire extinguisher?"

"What, Anthony? Tell me, because this should be good."

"Turner told me to pull it."

"Turner did no such thing."

Turner appeared behind Mike's head, in the window, making a frog face. He wagged his tongue.

"Turner told me that was how to get the fries to come up."

"If Turner told you to jump off a bridge, would you do it?"

"So you admit Turner could have lied to me?"

"Anthony, Turner is one of our most respected employees. You, on the other hand, have not been a model of good conduct. Do you understand? If some-one were to say to me, 'Is Anthony a model?' I would have to say: 'No. No, I'm afraid he's just not.' Now here's what I don't want to hear: You blaming every-thing on Turner. Because you're not supposed to be watching Turner. You're supposed to be watching Anthony. I don't know if what you say is true. I don't know whether it's false. But I do know that anyone who *paid attention*, do you get me? *Paid attention?* Anyone who paid attention would not be getting into the scrapes you do. Just like on the softball field. Am I understood?"

"Yes, but—"

"I see I'm not understood. Who is in charge of your drawer? You are. That's why it's named 'Your Drawer,' 'Anthony's Drawer,' okay? What goes into it and comes out of it is your business. A shortage or an overage is your business. Not Turner's. Not Rick's. Not Jenn's. Yours. You've got to keep your eyes open, Anthony. You've got to stop blaming your own problems on others. You could lose your job for wrongly accusing one of your fellow employees. I could fire you right now. I should. If I looked in the manual, it would probably say, 'Fire him.' But I won't fire you, Anthony. Why? Because I believe in you. I believe you can do better."

Mike opened the door.

"I'm giving you one more chance. You have two weeks to shape up. Keep your drawer balanced. And if you make this kind of accusation about a respected employee again, you'd better have some kind of evidence to back it up. Otherwise, Anthony, I'm sorry. I'm going to have to let you go. People are lining up for these jobs. There are women who have to support families. Men who have been injured while at a previous worksite. There are kids who want to pay for college. A lot of people, Anthony. They could all do your job, and do it better than you're doing it now. So get your head out of the clouds. Put your nose to the grindstone. Start concentrating on your own performance, not other people's. Is that understood?"

"Mike—"

"Understood?"

Finally, I nodded. "Yes, Mike. That's understood."

"Good," he said. "Now get out there and replenish the beverages."

I went. Mike closed the door.

That night, I wrote the next letter to Burger Queen. I sealed it. I stamped it. I sent it.

So far as I was concerned, the Plan was on again.

Chapter 5

. . . .

Try to get it all up. Nobody wants to see that," said Mike. He pointed at the floor. There was shake on the tiles. I nodded.

Mike said, "Are you still on for the game Saturday?"

"Yes," I said. "I'll be there."

"You're not a very strong hitter. Our best chance with you is if the pitcher walks you."

"I'm good at running."

"It's not a game of running. It's a game of hitting. But you're still a welcome addition to our team, Anthony. The different skills of different members of our O'Dermott's family complement each other to make us stronger. Everyone has a role to play."

"Thanks," I said.

"When you've cleaned that up, go into the back and get a carton of danish. We need to replenish the danish."

"Okay," I said.

Mike turned without a thank-you and walked away. I swabbed at the slime. It streaked pink and brown across the floor. I plunked the mop in the bucket. Foam from the shake drifted to the top of the water. The water was black. The foam was yellow.

"Hey, man," whispered Shunt. "Just dropped off the goods."

"What goods?"

"These goods." He pulled a sheaf of paper out of his jacket. "The script for the commercial they're shooting here."

"You stole it?"

"No. Dropped it off. I stole it yesterday. I made copies. Brought the original back just now while Mike and you were out here chewing the cud."

"You're insane!"

"Take a look."

I leaned the mop against the table. It slid to the side. I grabbed it and leaned it again. I took the script from Shunt. I read through part of it.

I pointed. "What's this?"

"I made a few little additions."

"I could never tell. They fit in seamlessly."

"Yeah," said Shunt. "That's the beauty of it."

• • •

O'Memo

From the Office of Charles Beaterson Tremlick, Director of Marketing

To: The Manager of O'Dermott's Franchise
#8423 (Billingston Main St.)
Re: Ad #DAA3

Dear Store Manager:

Congratulations on being selected for
inclusion in our new promotion—what we
like to call our "Dream Campaign." This
letter should serve to give you an idea of
the commercial that will include several
shots of your location.

The ad will consist of interspliced
scenarios emphasizing the important role
O'Dermott's plays in many aspects of our
customers' lives. Customers should think
of us as a valued friend, a business of
and for local people who really do care.

The scenes will include the following:
kids filing in after a soccer game; Kermit
O'Dermott rolling a promotional plastic
jalopy toward a granddaughter/grandfather
pair; two girls, high-school graduates,
laughing and throwing their mortarboards
up into the air; double-date situation
over shakes and fries; crowd applauding as
laughing baby takes its first steps into
Kermit O'Dermott's arms.

Jingle which will accompany the above action
is as follows:

<Introductory music rises, then:>

We've seen you laugh, we've seen you grow.
Your hopes, your dreams, your life we know.
And with the smiles and care we show
We hope to serve your dreams "to go."

Your dreams are ours. Your dreams are ours.
At O'Dermott's. Whooo-ha-hooo.

Our commitment's real and true
'Cuz you made us and we made you.
Good times and bad we've seen you through
Whatever you may be and do.
Our meat's uncooked and still goes "Moo".
You must like food that tastes like poo
And makes you want to retch and spew.
Your dreams are ours. Your dreams are ours.
At O'Dermott's. Whooo-ha-hooo.

Dreams of fun and dreams of friends.
Dreams of hope that never ends.
Dreams of a place where you can come
For food no matter where you're from.
Dreams of happy life transitions.
Dreams of underpaid positions.
Dreams with greasy nocturnal emissions
Laced with amaranth (E123), monosodium glutamate
Carageenan, traces of salmonella and campylobacter, potassium bromate
Sodium nitrite (a color fixative), not to mention synthetic antioxidants like BHA
(E320) and BHT (E321), and the various antibiotic compounds in our meat
And hormonal growth promoters like clenbuterol which make animals bulk up so unnaturally that they can't even stand on their own two / four underdeveloped feet. So. Who wants to eat?

• 117

"And which part did you write?"

"Guess."

"I couldn't possibly. You're a master."

"Please, guess."

"You're a master. How could I guess?"

"You'll learn. Subtlety is the thing."

"Anthony," Mike called from behind the counter, "you're on the clock. You're not paid to talk to Shunt. Conversation with Shunt can happen on your own time. Concentrate. Clean up the shake."

"Sorry," I said. "And then replenish the danish?"

"Yes," said Mike. "Then replenish the danish."

Jenn's suggestion that Rick and I go for a hike was a good one. The problem was, our schedules didn't work out. He was working the evening shift, and I was working the morning. Instead of a hike, we settled for a short walk. We went to the town forest. It wasn't a bad day. The humidity wasn't too high.

There was an old access road that was the best place to park. It was just gravel. Clover grew between the two tire tracks. Moss too. It led back into the center of the woods. We parked at the foot of Party Hill. There were tall pines there, going steeply up the slope. At the top were a few circles of rocks filled with old ashes and garbage. Party Hill was a part of nature that smelled like old beer.

At the foot of Party Hill was a wide pond. On the far bank, rushes grew.

This was where a lot of kids camped out or had their keggers. You always heard stories about the skinny-dipping, and how many virginities were lost in the bushes. There weren't, in fact, many bushes.

The night before the big commercial shoot, there was going to be a party here. It would not be sanctioned by O'Dermott's; Mike was turning a blind eye. We were having a party because everyone would have work off while the shoot was going on. Mike said that Management was going to come down for the shoot. Management had its own Staff. Management's Staff would do whatever Management needed. There would be no need for the regular employees. No one would work on those four days. No one would get paid. So we were having a party.

As Rick and I picked a path and went into the woods, we talked about the party, the ad, and the upcoming soft-ball game against Burger Queen. We walked around hills and hummocks.

The town forest had been farmland before the town bought it. There were still stone walls running through the woods. Occasionally, there were small stone founda-tions in the earth.

I felt bad that I hadn't seen Rick much since he got together with Jenn. Walking with him now, I remem-bered how smart he was, even if you had to stop him sometimes from climbing trees. He knew what was important to me.

He said gently, hanging from one arm about ten feet above the ground, "You're really messed up about this Diana thing."

"Yeah," I agreed.

"You confused?"

"Of course," I sighed.

"What's confusing?" he said. He let go and dropped. He crouched when he landed.

"Lots of complicated things."

"Like what? Turner being a wankbaron? That's not complicated."

"More like what I should have done."

"Done when?"

"To keep her interested."

We walked for a minute in silence. The forest was tall. Blue jays were screaming high above our hair.

Finally Rick said, "She thought you were great. She told Jenn she was way spun on you."

"She did?"

"Not in exactly those words. Jenn and I made up the 'way spun' thing last week when we were baking brownies together."

"So how did Diana's 'way spun' change into just friends?"

Rick thought about it for a minute. "I don't know." He suggested, "Maybe she was waiting for some passion."

"You're saying I didn't paw her up."

"You'd know better than me, man."

"Don't give me that. I respected her. That's the thing. I didn't want to be sleazy."

"Respect is fine, but there's got to be passion."

"There was passion."

"I'm telling you what I think." He started to climb another tree.

I faced the other way. My arms were crossed. "How can I be fun and interesting and still not be a draw?" I protested. His feet swung near my head. I said, "Girls already have to put up with enough people like sleazing all up on them. That's why respect is important. To quote the great Aretha, 'R-E-S-P-E-C-T. Find out what it means to me.'"

"Hey! Hey!" He pointed at me from the branch. "This is one of your problems. You're always Mr. Irony. You're never serious. You and Diana, completely sarcastic. Both of you."

"That's what I liked about her. That's what she liked about me. We didn't take anything for granted."

"Yeah, well maybe you were sarcastic a little too much. Love is no joke, man. Maybe that's something you should think about." He rustled around in the tree. "Sometimes it seemed like you and Diana were making fun of Jenn and me."

"That's not true. No way."

"Well, Jenn's great. The thing about Jenn is . . . man, I think there's some kind of animal living in this thing."

"Would you get out of there? I can't talk to someone who's upside-down."

"All the blood's going right to my head."

He pulled himself right side up and climbed down. We kept walking.

I said, "Everyone expects you to force yourself on people. To be like, 'Hey, baby. I like the way you flap your hinterlands.'"

"I don't think anybody expects you to say 'hinterlands.'"

"Yeah, okay. To do some obnoxious come-on. But if you act on your desires, you're gross. And if you do the opposite, act like Mr. Nice Guy, then you're a weenie."

"You're saying there's no way you can be."

"Well, there is, there's two ways—gross or weenie."

He thought for a minute, then said, "It wasn't very clear sometimes what Diana wanted."

"No," I agreed. "What exactly do you mean by that?"

He didn't answer. We walked beside the river. Both of us kept an eye out for turtles. On the far side of the river, some people were building houses with three-car garages. The windows were just holes. The outsides were covered with paper.

"Jenn and I are thinking about doing it," he said suddenly.

"You've talked about it?"

"Yeah," he said. "We'd be making out, and it would come up."

"Mm-hm."

"So we're going to. I don't know, you know? Maybe I'm kind of forcing it, but you've got to talk about what you want. I mean, that's what it's all about, isn't it? That's what they want, women, us talking about our feelings, you know? So, I'm like, well, this is what I want; why hide it? I'm like, 'Come on. We're ready for this.' And she's all, 'I don't know. I'm kind of frightened. I don't know.' So I was like, 'Someday we'll be old or maybe dead and then we'll have missed our chance.' Then I started to lay it on about like worms eating our guts and moss growing over our faces. That convinced her."

"You really are a charmer," I granted him.

"I guess I'll probably buy her like roses or some nice cactuses or something to get her ready. We'll go someplace good for dinner."

"In the paper there's a two-for-one coupon at Friendly's."

"Rockin'."

"So you've thought about it."

"Thought about what?"

"Like, this whole question of what to do about sex. Whether it's weak to give in to your johnson just because it wakes you up screaming."

Rick shook his head. "Man, I don't want to visit your brain."

"I keep wondering. The other day I asked Shunt whether he thought it was stronger to give in and do it or to control yourself."

"Yeah? What did he say?"

"He grabbed my hair, pulled my head over, and yelled into my ear, *'Attention, moron: Resist the chemicals.'*"

"Shunt's a freak."

"I always worried about this with Diana."

"Look. The way I figure it, you can't think about this kind of thing too much." As we walked through a field with lots of yellow spiders, he said, "We're talking about passion here. You don't want to be a dripster. Don't think. You think too much. Don't. It's about passion, man. You can't ask questions about passion." His voice filled with a runny, sticky kind of golden sunlight. "Passion is like—something beyond all other . . ." He waved his hands. ". . . things. Passion is about true love. When you're in love—I mean, like Jenn and me are—I'm talking truly in love—and you care deeply about a person—what could be wrong? When there's not a minute of the day when you aren't wanting to be with them, lying on the couch, watching videos, and kissing, and feeling them up, and fooling around with them. I think about her all the time. That's true love."

We had reached the high concrete wall in the woods where someone had spray-painted:

GUYS SUCK

There was an apostrophe painted out in another color.

"You'll understand someday," said Rick, standing under the huge "GUYS SUCK." "When you've really felt true love. I mean, eternal. The way that a man can love a woman. Then you'll know what I'm talking about."

Looking at the wall made me sad. I thought about Diana's shoulder pressed next to mine. Someone's size ten sneakers rotting on our shoulders. Wondering whether we would kiss the first time. I turned around. Rick was sizing up the trees. We started away from the wall in the woods. We went down a hill. Someone had strung up a wire between two trees, like they were trying to kill a motorbiker. We stopped and tried to take it down. We couldn't without tools.

Later we came upon the ruined house in the woods. Rick wanted to go in and look around. I said no, it was dangerous. I didn't want him to find the troll. I said, "Let's go back."

On the way back to the car, we made up stories about what was buried in the foundation.

The day of the softball game against Burger Queen, it was raining. I had to start work at six in the morning. It had been raining all night. Business was very slow. The rain washed down the windows in waves. When Rick came in at seven-thirty, he was angry.

"Rained out. Can you believe it? This sucks vastly." I didn't care. I was so sleepy I could hardly stand up.

At around ten, Mike arrived.

"Sorry about the rain, boys," he said. "This is a time when we all just need to be patient. There's always next week."

He went into the back to make a phone call. A few minutes later, he came out. He looked confused.

"I just talked to them over at Burger Queen," he said. "The game's on."

Rick shook his head. "Have they looked outside?"

"It's their prerogative," said Mike. "They're the home team."

When my shift was over, I went into the back and slept for about twenty minutes. It was the early afternoon. The game was at three. I changed. Rick gave me a ride. The rain beat down so hard Rick had his windshield wipers on high. They whacked back and forth. The field was right behind some new condos. I had played soccer on it several years before. It had been fine then.

When we got there, we were surprised. Apparently, when they built Riverview Estates, they had blocked up the river. It had overflowed. The field was a broad pond. The BQ team was already warming up, ankle-deep in water. The O'Dermott's players were just getting there. Two of them had thought the game was off, and had spent the morning getting baked and watching cartoons. Turner drove up in his Oldsmobile. There was a girl at his side. She had her arm around him. He got out, patted the car, and kissed its roof. She laughed.

"Who's that?" I asked Rick.

"I don't know. I think her name's Stacey. She's Turner's girlfriend."

"Hm," I said. "I didn't know he had a girlfriend."

"It's strange but true."

Shunt arrived on his bicycle. He wasn't scheduled to play. He was wearing black jeans, some chains, and an old cheerleader's skirt. The skirt was looking kind of moth-eaten and torn. The BQ team started laughing at him. Shunt walked up to their center fielder and grimaced. He head-butted the center fielder, and the center fielder went down. Luckily, it was raining too hard for anyone to notice.

Mike's wife was standing in a pink raincoat holding a polka-dotted blue see-through umbrella. Her double-stroller was under the umbrella. Mike was on the pitcher's mound, yelling at BQ's captain and the ump. We went over to hear.

"I call this substandard!" Mike waved his hand around the field. The current made little ripples around his legs. "We do not have to stand for this lack of drainage!"

The BQ captain grinned. "Hey, our team is ready to play. Of course, we've been practicing here for several weeks, so maybe we're just used to playing ankle-deep in water. But we're ready to go."

"You cannot seriously expect us to play on this field," said Mike to the umpire.

The umpire looked around. "What's the problem? You want to forfeit?"

"Forfeit?" cried Mike. "We should not have to forfeit!"

"Home team calls the fitness of the field. Captain, your assessment?"

The BQ captain said, "Looks fine to me. Looks like it has every afternoon for oh, the past three weeks."

"You've been practicing every day for three weeks? This is supposed to be a casual game!" Mike turned to the umpire. "You have got to call the game on account of rain."

The ump shook his head. "Correction: I don't *got* to do anything."

"You've been paid off, haven't you?"

"No comment."

"They paid you off."

"Is your team going to forfeit?" said the umpire. "Just tell me now."

"No we are not going to forfeit!" said Mike.

"Ho-key-doh-key," said the ump slowly. He shrugged and walked away.

BQ's captain wriggled and smiled. "This'll get you back for the troll."

Mike looked confused. "I'm confused. What troll? What troll would this be you're talking about?"

The BQ captain nodded. "Sure. You know nothing. O'Dermott's knows nothing. That's fine, Mike. Keep playing that game. Meanwhile, we'll whup your asses at this one."

He walked away from us. He looked confident.

Mike stared after him. Suddenly, he knelt. He put his hands under the water. He ran them along the ground. He looked up and called after the BQ captain, "Hey, this isn't grass! This isn't even grass, but some kind of lake weed!"

I was not in the starting lineup. That made me grateful. That meant I could just stand in the rain without moving for a couple of innings. Just until one of the starters developed pneumonia and had to go get a tracheotomy.

There were no bleachers. Apparently they had washed downriver a couple of years before. The bleachers were now sitting behind the junk lot at Ray Gormagan's Autobody and Parts, as if rust were a spectator sport.

We stood in clumps on a slope. Some people had umbrellas. Not many people came just to watch the game. Rick wouldn't go under an umbrella. He said that would be weak. He had on a cap. He had four little rivers spitting constantly off his visor. Shunt didn't seem to mind the rain. He danced around in it and howled.

The first inning didn't go well. Turner hit a double

with no one on base. No one brought him home. The BQ team didn't talk much or make fun of us. They didn't need to. There was laughter in their eyes. Turner was furious. He stood there way out in the field of water. He shifted from leg to leg near the floating milk carton that marked second. He looked uncomfortable.

It wasn't long before they were up. Turner pitched. They were good pitches. They were fast and angry. That didn't stop BQ from getting two runs.

The next inning was worse. My teeth were chattering. Listening to the other team talk, I started to realize that they had made playing in water a basic part of their game. They had adapted. They figured the current into their batting and fielding. They had a special language.

"Go for it, Fletcher! Gargle on third!"

"Diveball to center field!"

"Yo, Webster! Periscope up!"

There was only one person on our side who didn't seem to notice the game was underwater. Mike's wife. She was very peppy. She was always clapping and yelling, "Go OD's! Go, Emerald Ovals! Go, go, go O'Dermott's!" When there was a quiet moment on the field, she would lean down to the stroller and coo, "'O'Dermott's.' Can you say that? Clap your widdy hands. 'Go, O'Dermott's! Go, Daddy! Go, best daddy in the world!' Say it!"

When people dived for bases, they were almost half underwater. The ball smacked into the water and rolled. One of our fielders' gloves was coming apart. The leather was wet. The score by the end of the fourth inning was 6-1. Mike tromped up and down, his cuffs heavy with water. His hands were shaking with rage. Our players stood with their shoulders slumped and their equipment dragging. Their hair stuck down straight from their caps. Shunt was cavorting. He'd grabbed clumps of lake weed for pom-poms. He was calling out letters of the alphabet for people to give him. No one gave him the letters he wanted. People just glared at him. The letters all spelled names of places in South and Central America which had been clear-cut by beef suppliers. He and Mike's wife were the only two egging the team on.

"Go, O'Dermott's! Go, Emerald Ovals!" she would say.

"Go, multibillion-dollar, multinational corporations!" Shunt would add, clasping his hands together. "Go, go, *go* hypocritical murderers bent on world domination!"

"Hi, you must be Stacey," I said to Turner's girlfriend. She was blonde, with very complicated hair.

"Yeah," she said, flinching her nostrils.

"Turner's always talking about you."

"I hate to think."

"No, only good things. Only good things! Well, of course, you know Turner: It isn't *only* good things. But it's *mostly* good things. I mean, mostly things that are *pretty* good. Sometimes. You know how he is."

"A jerk?"

"Yeah." There was an awkward silence. She was waiting for me to say something. At this point, I realized I didn't have anything else to say. I didn't know how far I could go bashing Turner before she told him. So I rocked on my heels. I tried: "Great day for a ball game, huh?"

She shook her head. "This is so gross. I can't believe they did this to you guys."

"It's like really raining."

"Yeah, and the river and all."

"There's an octopus in the dugout."

She looked around. "Where's the dugout?"

"Uh, no," I said. "There is no dugout. That was a joke."

"Yeah, thanks. I knew it was a joke, I thought there might just be a dugout, that's all."

"No."

"You'd drown, anyway."

"Yeah."

"Do you play for the team?"

"Badly," I admitted.

"It's a stupid game, anyway," she said.

"It sure is," I said.

"Like why do you want to hit a stupid ball with a bat?"

"A piece of wood," I agreed. "Hitting a little pouch of leather and rubber with a stick."

"Really dumb," she said. "What's it ever done to you?" She laughed at her joke.

"Exactly," I said. "Now you're talking."

"Sorry to be so like negative."

"You can say whatever you want. Doesn't Turner let you say whatever you want with him? I mean, I personally am all for people saying whatever they feel like saying."

She looked at me from under her hair. "You hitting on me?" she asked.

"Ack—!" I said. "What do you—? What? Am I—? Am I hitting on you? No. Got to go." This seemed like a really good way to get my butt whipped fast. I was out of there like a shot.

"Anthony," said Mike. "Top of the sixth, you're in."

"As what?"

"Substitution for Lee. Right field."

"Are you sure you want me to go in?" I asked, looking at the water.

Mike shrugged. "It doesn't matter now. At this point, we're just playing to play," he said miserably.

Now I was nervous. I looked around the field. I recognized several of the guys from BQ who had beaten me up. Kid was the catcher. Things were not looking good. After five innings, the score was 8-2.

I was late in the lineup. Our first batter struck out. The second one popped the first pitch right to the third baseman. The rain kept up. Turner flied out. He threw down the bat and yelled things. Mike cautioned him about language.

We had to go out onto the field. I walked down the final few feet of slope before the water started. I splashed out to right field. The muck oozed in my shoes.

The second I got on the field, I could feel the anger. Out there, there was no protection. My team was full of hatred. The other team was full of spite. All of it was raw. Nobody was pretending.

Turner scowled on the mound, but it didn't do any

good. He wasn't used to the drag of the water. His pitches were lame. The ump called several balls. Then BQ's batters started to connect. Johnny Fletcher whacked a long, high fly to center field. Webster hit a grounder to the mound. He brought Fletcher home.

Marston stepped up to bat.

Mike yelled, "Anthony! Play him deep! Play him deep!" He waved his hands as if shoving me backward.

"Deep meaning what?" I yelled. "Twenty-thousand fathoms?" Nobody laughed. I backed up.

Marston bunted.

Everyone swore. People just wanted to quit. There was a little dispute, because the ball washed into foul territory. The ump was on their side. They got the runs. Turner looked angry, or like he was about to cry.

It was at about this time that I looked up and saw some girls arriving in a station wagon. I knew Diana had been hanging out with some of the girls from BQ and Wendy's. I couldn't make out faces through the rain. Something was happening to my left.

"The ball! Stop gawking! You have got to think, Anthony! Concentrate!" Mike yelled.

The ball was dribbling out past me. Too late.

I stood, dripping and defeated. Silt washed through my boxers.

By the time we were up again, the score was 13-2. I was determined to do something heroic before she left. It didn't look like she was going to be staying long. She and the other girls watched the game, but they didn't look very interested. It looked like they were just there to switch cars or pick some people up.

The top of the seventh did not start very well. The first batter struck out. The second batter popped a fly right to first. I was milling around on the shore. I tried to wander in her direction to hear what they were talking about. Mike saw me.

"Anthony!" he said. "Where the heck are you going? Where is your team spirit? Explanation as to why you aren't watching? Explanation as to why you're lost in your own world? Explanation as to why I should give you the chance I'm giving you?" She heard my name and looked over. I stood and concentrated on the catcher's back. Rick and Turner were up, then me. I was already feeling weak and nervous.

Rick drove a single to left field. Turner stepped up to bat, gritting his teeth. I could tell he was mad. The BQ pitcher was Johnny Fletcher, who worked window. Fletcher was teasing Turner. He sent Turner pitches which were high and slow. They had a weird spin, almost dainty. Turner was covered in mud. I could hear him swearing. On the third pitch, he finally swung and connected.

"Go, O'Dermott's!" yelled Mike's wife. "Go, go, green!"

The ball shot past the right fielder's shoulder. He splashed after it. The ball thwacked into the water. Turner slogged to first. The fielder was scrabbling way off in the outfield. Turner was kicking up a spray somewhere around second. Rick had made it to third. He had just started home when the ball flew back into the infield and smacked into Fletcher's wet glove. Rick turned and hurled himself back toward third. He came up choking and wheezing. The third baseman had caught the ball. Rick's eyes were wide and he was hiccupping.

"Player's choking!" yelled the ump.

"You choking?" asked the third baseman. Rick couldn't answer.

"Use the Heimlich maneuver!" yelled the BQ coach.

"That a play?" asked the third baseman.

"No! You grab him around near the ribs, like this!"

Rick gagged and thrashed his arms.

The third baseman caught on and went to help Rick. Rick was gargling. The third baseman went to wrap his arms around Rick's torso. Rick saw the ball in the glove and backed off, choking. He thrashed one hand in the water, and with the other, grabbed at the buoy that marked third. He fell, and writhed backward.

"What's the matter?" yelled the ump.

"He's running away. I think he's trying to make sure he's safe."

The ump trudged over. "Is he touching the base?"

Fletcher asked, "Is the ball still in play?"

Mike screamed, "Would you just declare the boy safe before he drowns to death?"

The ump shrugged. "Ho-key-doh-key. Safe!"

"Now give him the Heimlich maneuver!" said the BQ captain.

It just took a minute before Rick was spewing water. His face turned back from red.

I was up. Everyone glowered at me. They were not happy about Mike's lineup. Men on second and third, two outs, and I was up. This didn't look good to anyone.

Fletcher smiled at me like a wolf or some other cruel pack animal. I turned and looked for Diana. She was watching.

"Strike one!" the ump called.

"Would you concentrate?" Mike roared. "For once?"

Fletcher caught the ball and wound up. He threw it again. I swung.

"Strike two!"

Turner started yelling from second base. "Come on, you little pansy! You little shit! Would you do something right for once? Hit the goddamn ball! Just hit the god-damn ball!"

"Language!" said Mike.

"Umpire," said Fletcher. "I can't possibly concentrate with all this bickering."

"Right," said the ump. "Runners should shut their gobs."

Turner watched me with hatred.

Fletcher wound up again. He threw it. I swung.

And connected. It seemed so easy, now that I had done it. The connection was firm. The ball went flying. I ran as hard as I could. I didn't even look toward Diana. As I splashed down the base line, I thought to myself, *I'm just concentrating on running, not looking at all for Diana or getting distracted by other things.*

I rounded first and headed for second. I didn't even allow myself to look up.

I had therefore almost gotten to third before the third baseman told me Fletcher had caught the ball on the fly and I had been out for some time.

That was three outs. Then BQ was up. It just kept going on. I don't remember the details. I plunged after a ball or two. Fletcher hit a homer. When Turner pitched, Kid didn't budge his bat. Kid made a big show of yawning. He struck out on purpose. I wasn't very aware of what was going on. Finally they were saying it was over. They were saying the score was 20-2. People were swearing. That was it.

I walked back toward the slope. I was soaked. I was shivering. Kid and Fletcher were talking to Turner.

"Great final inning," Fletcher said to Turner.

"Don't mess with us," Kid said.

Fletcher added, "This'll teach you O'Dermott's girls not to steal."

Kid said, "Any time you want to apologize and give it back—"

"You can kiss our butts," Fletcher finished.

"What the hell you talking about?"

Kid and Fletcher looked at each other. "Sure, Turner," Kid said. "Keep playing dumb. You seem like a natural."

They walked away. Turner saw me. I changed direction. It wasn't fast enough. He caught me.

The first few times underwater weren't so bad. I'd managed to catch my breath soon after he grabbed my hair. I was very calm and blew out through my nose. There was a stick in the water, and I was afraid it would put my eye out. I could feel how soft my eye was. Each time my head slammed into the water, the stick reared up toward my eye. I tried to splutter that he couldn't push me so deep, that it was really dangerous. The next time I went down, I got water in my mouth. I started gagging. It tasted earthy. It stung inside my nose.

He kicked me in the spine. I curled up in the water. The stick was digging into my cheek. I wrapped my hands around my knees. My whole body ached. Turner was walking away. Just behind him, I saw Diana, watching us without moving, like it was someone's funeral. The next time I looked, she was gone.

I stood up. My body was soaked. I climbed the hill.

Rick was getting ready to leave. I had to catch a ride with him. He had put down towels on his car seats. I was about to get in when I saw Shunt quietly unlocking his bike.

"Shunt!" I called. He looked up. "Where are you going?"

He looked at me like I was crazy. "The bushes."

"You can't go to the bushes in this rain," I said. "The bushes will be flooded."

"I have a piece of plastic."

"Don't go to the bushes, man. It's like fifty degrees and pouring."

"The bushes are fine."

"I bet my parents would let you stay on the sofa. It's a sofa bed. It folds out."

"Is something wrong with the bushes?"

"It's pouring! Won't you just find a friend and stay at their house? You can't stay out in this!"

Shunt shook his head. He got on his bike. "Yeah, thanks, but screw you, Mom," he said, and started to ride off. "See you later."

Rick looked after him like he was diseased. I got in the car and closed the door.

Rick drove me home. He didn't say anything about the fact that I had lost him his run. He didn't say anything at all. He let me out of the car almost without talking. I stood there as he drove away. I had a coughing fit.

I went inside to take a shower. I was glad I had a Plan.

The next day, Mike gave me photocopied signs that explained to our patrons we would be closed the next four days on account of a commercial. He told me that we needed to keep the place spick-and-span, more than usual. He told me to look smart, by which he meant snappy. He explained he needed the signs taped to all the doors. He was worried about Management coming.

He gave me a roll of tape. It was a weighted dispenser. I went from door to door. I spooled out lengths of tape and ran my finger along them to fasten them to the corners of the paper. I hung them inside so they looked out.

At one point I got the tape caught on myself. Then I got it caught on an announcement. Then I got the announcement caught on myself. I was clutching the other announcements under my arm. My arm was folded like a chicken wing. I reached my head down to bite the tape. It didn't tear.

I knelt down and dropped the flyers. They fanned out

across the floor. I put down the tape. I pulled it off my shirt. I tried to peel it off the announcement. The announcement tore. The letters were the first things to go. I crumpled up the announcement and threw it in the trash. Then I started to gather up the other announcements from the floor.

I heard Turner yelling, "Dudes! About time. Where you been?"

I had all the flyers in my hands. I tapped them on the tiles to make their edges straight.

"Can't hear you, man," said one of the guys. "You'll have to speak up."

"Excuse me? Excuse me?" said another. They were the two guys we'd gone to the graveyard with.

"What the hell you been doing?" Turner said. "And what the hell's that?"

"Can't hear you, man. Please talk into the microphone."

"Periscope up," said the other.

They were right on the other side of some plastic plants and trash barrels. I heard a rustling and looked up fearfully. A long metal stalk poked up over the plants. It had a box for a head.

"What is that thing?" asked Turner. "Where you been?"

"We're not going to take that BQ bull."

"No way," said the other one. "Picking that field? No way are we gonna take that. Them like paying off the ump? No way."

"So we just had a little payback."

"What?" said Turner. I could hear the excitement in his voice. "What'd you guys do?"

"So we swung by the Burger Queen—"

"Home of the Jumbo."

"No," said Turner. "That's my pants."

"Swung by BQ, pulled up in back."

"The drive-thru lane."

"Drove right up to the microphone."

"Right up."

"Stole it."

There was a silence.

"The microphone. Which is what we—"

"Taa-daa!"

"—have right here."

"That's theirs?" Turner hissed. "Man, you have to hide that thing! Mike sees that, we're dead! Why'd you bring it in?"

"You'll have to speak into the microphone."

"Hi, Turner. Can we take your order?"

"Please proceed to the first window."

"Shut the hell up," said Turner. "Get that out of here!"

"Periscope up!" said one of them.

The plastic ferns wagged. Suddenly the square head of the microphone thrust through again. It stared down at me. I flattened myself against the trash barrel. The head jiggled. It was dented.

"Stop screwing around!" said Turner.

The head pulled back.

"Are you pissed off or something?" said one of them.

"'Course I'm pissed off!" said Turner. "You're a couple of idiots! Why didn't you take me with you? I'd've gone, man."

"It was kind of a spur of the minute thing."

"We were just like, hey, we could throw a rock at their camera and then grab their microphone."

"You broke the camera?"

"That'll teach 'em to laugh at my goddamn game."

"We had to break the camera, man. Otherwise they would've seen us hitting the microphone with the softball bats."

"BANG! BANG! And it was like, *wiggle, wiggle, wiggle. Wiggle, wiggle, wiggle.*"

"Stop waving that thing around. Jeez, you girls are stupid. Mike sees this, he'll be completely ripped and he'll call the cops."

"So what do you think of it?"

"It's risky, man," said Turner, "but necessary. I mean, you got to do what you got to do."

"Exactly."

"Thank you for such a great game, Mrs. BQ. BANG! BANG! BANG!"

"It wasn't all them," said Turner. "I was on sucky form."

"Yeah. We shouldn't have gotten stoked before the game."

"We didn't play too good either."

"You sucked," said Turner. "And that little shit whatsisname—Little Miss Anthony—" (my fingers tightened on my knees) "—he sucked bigtime. After the game I kicked him so hard he was puking. I like held his head underwater. He was gasping for breath and stuff. I said, 'That'll show you to mess up my game.' Then I put his head under again for a really long time. And gentlemen, it felt beautiful."

"Please, Turner. Just once. Speak into the mike."

When I got home, my parents were sitting holding hands in the den. The den was dark. The day wasn't bad outside, but the shades were drawn.

"Hey," I said, and started up the stairs.

"Anthony," said my father.

"Darling," said my mother. "We need to talk." She had a legal notepad next to her on the sofa.

My hand was on the banister. "What's up?"

"Why don't you take a seat in that chair?" my father said sorrowfully. "It's very comfortable."

I walked over to the recliner. I was suspicious. I sat down slowly. "Should I extend the footrest?"

My father shook his head. My mother said, "Anthony."

I wriggled. I wanted to center myself on the cushion. It seemed like it might be the kind of conversation where you wanted to be in the center of the cushion.

"Anthony," said my mother. She took a deep breath, and let it all out. Her cheeks inflated when she sighed. "We heard about Diana."

I felt a quick sense of panic. "Heard what about her?"

"That she . . . Anthony, you know."

"How she . . . ," said my father. He waved his hand in the air.

My mother consulted her pad. "Someone named Turner? At a party?"

"She . . . ," said my father. He waved his hand more.

My mother said, "There was chemistry between them?"

I stood up. "Who told you?"

"That doesn't matter, Anthony," said my mother, putting out her arms. "Oh, my little baby. I hate to see you hurt inside."

"It does matter."

"Anthony," said my father, rising to his feet. "There's nothing as bad as losing a woman you love."

My mother said, "I think it's about time for a family hug."

"Who told you about this?" I demanded. My mother and father were intertwining, holding out their arms to me. My mother tried to take me by the upper arm.

"Don't touch me! Stop!" I shook them off.

"Anthony," said my mother, "you can't let it bother you just because Diana fooled around with some jerk."

"This is none of—"

"Mrs. Gravitz told us, honey. I guess she overheard some things."

My father said, "By God, Anthony, I know how it is to lose a good woman." For a minute, he just sucked on his teeth. He shook his head. "Anthony, if she left you, she just wasn't worthy of you."

"That's not true," I said. "That's just not true."

"We thought she was pretty special, too," said my mother, nodding. "But sometimes you can be wrong about a person."

"You'll get over this sooner than you expect," said my father. "This is what the teenage years are all about. It may seem like a disaster right now. But Anthony, remember: There are always other fish in the sea."

"Thanks, Pop. That sounds like a great dating option."

"You know what I mean."

"I'll just fill the car with brine and cruise."

"There's no need to be sarcastic with your father."

"This is none of your business."

"Stop fighting us," said my mother, smoothing the hairs on my arm with her hand. "Let the grieving process start."

"It sounds like Diana was a little fast for you," said my father. "It's too bad, because I liked that girl. I liked that girl a whole heap of a lot."

I pulled my arm away. "This is none of your business!"

"Come on, Anthony," said my mother. "Let's make a cup of cocoa and some cookies together. It will be just like old times."

"It's the—it's—it's the middle of the summer!" I spluttered. "I will not have any cocoa! This is none of your—!"

I ran out the door.

I hated him. Turner. I hated him for all the shame. I hated him for what people thought. What people knew. I hated him because he'd taken her away. I walked through the 'burbs. It looked like rain. I walked all the way to the car park where we'd had our picnic.

I started the walk up and down. I walked in circles. I walked through the levels. I saw the rain start in the air shaft. I saw it speckle the pavement on the top level. It made the tarmac smell hot and dusty.

I walked until late in the night. The rain was quiet, as if healing. I went to a phone. I dialed a number. It was Burger Queen.

"Hello," I said. "This is a friend." Through the phone, I heard the rattle of trays. In a voice low and strange, I said, "I have some information about your troll."

Chapter 6

. . . .

I hid behind a tree. I was not close to the fire.

There were three stumps around me. All of them were big with moss. My knee pressed into one of them. The moss was cool and wet. I worried about what might be slithering there. Bugs love to live in moss.

The tree was a beech. My fingers curled around it. They kept me steady. I was squatting. No one could see me.

Shunt and I had finished our secret errand. Everything was in place. Tonight was the night. The Plan would bear fruit. Stage three. Everything was perfect. When we had finished preparing, Shunt had gone and joined the party. I had to wait. We wanted to throw people off the scent by arriving separately.

Music came from the top of Party Hill. People were shouting at each other and laughing. I didn't recognize the music. It had a lush guitar sound. It wasn't bad. Somewhere up there, there was a keg, maybe two. I could see the flames of the bonfire. Quick, dark shapes threw themselves around the fire, between the tangle of boughs.

Below, I could see the pond reflecting the black outline of the forest. Above, I could see the hills that started a few miles north, rising to the mountains in the next state. There was a dim, sick haze where the strip malls lay.

It had been about fifteen minutes. Time for me to go up.

I walked casually up the path.

The party was in full swing. People were sitting on logs. People were sloshing beer around in cups. Turner manned the keg. A few guys and a girl stood next to the CD player, pointing to different CDs, bickering. They couldn't agree on what to play. I recognized almost everyone from O'Dermott's. Jenn and Rick were by the fire, both with beers. They waved. I saw Stacey, Turner's girlfriend, standing to one side of them, looking out of place.

I went over to them. A plan about Stacey was forming itself in my head. I thought it was important to impress her.

"Hey, guys," I said, to Rick and Jenn.

"Hi, Anthony."

"Hey."

There was a silence. We looked at each other expectantly. We had run out of things to say.

"So," Rick tried. "I brought my brother along tonight."

"Good. Great."

"I thought it might be fun for him."

We looked around for Rick's brother. We finally saw

him near two kissing couples. Their backs were brushing him. He was standing with both hands over his face, trembling.

"Oh," said Rick, without much enthusiasm. "There he is over there."

There was another awkward silence. I worried that Stacey was listening. We stood and looked at the fire. It had been made of lots of broken boughs, the remains of a go-cart, and charcoal.

"That's a big fire," I said, not knowing what else to say. Jenn and Rick were in their own little love-continent.

"They started it with gasoline," said Jenn.

"There was a big old explosion."

"I thought they were going to take out some owls."

"It looked like something from hell."

Jenn raised her finger. "Smokey the Bear says," and they both recited in furry voices, "'Only you can prevent forest fires.'"

From there they moved on to, "Give a hoot! Don't pollute!" and for a little bit we made up our own. "Don't leave a log! Just curb your dog!" "Please, boys and girls. Don't bite our squirrels." "Psychos and townies! Don't bury Brownies!" and so on.

I happened to glance at Stacey. She was smiling.

"Sorry for listening in," she said.

"Uh, no," I said, smiling widely, trying to think up something to say. "No, that's, well, fine."

We all stared at the fire. The burning go-cart had been steered by means of a cable.

"Where's Turner?" I asked Stacey, knowing the

answer. "Oh, over there near the keg. Didn't he intro-
duce you to anyone?"

She shook her head. "Nope. He figured I could meet
people myself."

"I just cannot believe he left you alone," I said, shaking
my head. "That's a damn shame. I certainly wouldn't
have."

Rick cleared his throat to one side of me.

Stacey smiled a secret smile at me.

Okay, I thought. *I am on the way to paying Turner back. This
would be the icing on the cake. Above and beyond the Plan. An
extra bonus. So keep up the charm.*

"Your hair always looks so complicated," I said.

"Is that a nice thing to say?"

"How do you make hair that complicated?"

"It takes a while."

"Do you use rivets?"

She looked at me like I was insane. Rick and Jenn
excused themselves.

Rick said, "Niffer and I are going over to get some
more beer." He pointed at Jenn when he said "Niffer."

"We really want to drink," said Jenn.

"We're going for twerped."

They walked off arm-in-arm, giggling. I could
tell they were giggling about the fact I was flirting
with Stacey.

"They're so cute," I said.

"Eeuw," she said.

"You should have met them before the lobotomies."

She laughed a little. "You're not really normal, are
you?" she said.

I hesitated. "How would you like me to answer that question?"

"You're working too hard," she said. "Just try and be like normal."

"What will happen if I'm normal enough?" I raised my eyebrows.

"See? That's sleazy. Try again. Like try asking me where I'm from."

I asked her. She said Chester. This was going swimmingly. She asked where I was from. I said Billingston.

"Now talk about the towns," she said. "Billingston's pretty nice."

"Yeah," I said, shrugging. "It's okay. It's kind of boring."

"Chester's wicked boring."

"More boring than Billingston?"

"Chester's farther from the city."

"Yeah," I said. "But you have the mall."

"See?" she said, patting me on the shoulder. "Now we're having like this completely normal conversation."

"Can I stop for a question?"

"Yeah. Shoot."

"Is Turner going to strip the skin off my body for talking to you?"

"There you go off the like—you're off the deep end again. And I don't care what Turner does."

"I do. He can hurt a person."

"Look, can I talk to you? Completely serious?" She glanced at Turner. He was in a T-shirt, still dishing out the beer.

"Sure. I mean—sure."

"Really. No jokes."

"No jokes."

"I know you're Turner's friend, but you know he can be a real jerk?"

I nodded in deep understanding. "It must be difficult for you, Stacey."

"I said lay off it. Here's the thing: I heard some rumor earlier tonight."

"What's that?"

"I heard he'd made it or at least fooled around with some burger bitch. That true?"

I felt myself blushing. "There was—who do you—I mean—"

"It's true, isn't it? Some party last month? She held the pickle, held the lettuce?"

"Well . . . that's . . . that's a Burger Queen slogan," I corrected.

"Look. You may be his friend, but I deserve to know."

I nodded. I pressed my hands together, palm to palm. "Yeah," I said. "He fooled around with someone."

Stacey twisted up her mouth. She looked around the ring of fire. People were standing. People were slipping. People were slumped near each other. A few were dancing. Turner was shouting at the music people. He had musical suggestions.

"Okay," said Stacey. "Which one of them? Tell me which one."

"None of them here."

"Come on. Point her out to me."

"She's not here. I'm telling you."

"You think I'm gonna believe that?"

"It's the truth. Turner was so mean to her afterward she quit."

"Quit completely?"

"Yeah. She was completely . . ." I didn't have anything else to say. I didn't want to tell Stacey that the burger bitch had been my girlfriend. I didn't want her to know Turner had taken Diana away from me. I didn't want to look like a loser.

She searched my face, waiting.

I pointed at the air, where the music was. "Meatloaf," I said. "The *Bat Out of Hell* album. I bet it's been a really long time since that last echoed through these woods."

"Unfortunately not," she said, crossing her arms and throwing herself back against a tree. "It's Turner's favorite."

He was coming over. He had a big, uneven grin on his face. I stepped back from her. She noticed him coming. She straightened up. She touched her hair.

"Got to go," I said.

Turner tossed back some beer. He filled his cheeks with it. His cheeks grew and shrank as he squirted the beer in and out of his teeth. He tossed his plastic cup into the woods. There was an arc of yellow beer behind it, shining in the firelight.

He was beside us. "Talking to Little Miss Wussy?" he said.

"He's more interesting than you," she said, touching her clothes to make sure they hung right.

"Interesting isn't everything. Could I have this dance, lady?"

I backed out. Some guys in untucked plaid ran past me. Turner and Stacey were clasping hands. I went to talk to Shunt.

He was perched on a log like a gargoyle.

"Shunt," I said.

"So far, so good."

"Any time now," I said.

He grinned. "They won't know what hit 'em."

I wanted to talk more about the Plan, but we couldn't. Some girls came over. We had to shoot the breeze. The girls ate hotdogs they'd burned on the fire. Turner and Stacey were dancing. Jenn and Rick were playing finger games and drinking as fast as they could. People ran into each other. Guys and girls made out in the dirt. Rick's brother wandered among them gently. He surveyed each of their faces like an alien trying to understand lilies. Their faces were streaked. He watched their hands scrape through each other's hair. The guys had to stop and shift their pants. Shunt was talking to the girls about O'Dermott's meat suppliers. He took the hotdogs out of the girls' hands and made the hotdogs into toys. The hotdogs snorted and squealed and kissed one another.

"To stun a pig?" Shunt said. "Takes about one point three amps. Any less and they feel everything while they're slaughtered. Paralyzed but not unconscious as they're cut apart. O'Dermott's meat suppliers for the sausage patties use about point forty-five amps. Our little porkers are able to feel the whole show." He handed back the weiners. "Like some ketchup with that?"

Jenn and Rick played rock/paper/scissors. They

chugged. Several of the older employees who had lost their brains—dropped them or burned them up—sometime in the early seventies, were gathered in a group. They smiled at all us youth. They were toking. The heavy, sweet smell was everywhere. Shunt had frightened off the girls. He went into the woods to be alone.

Rick and Jenn were sweaty. They danced. I watched them. They grabbed hands and pumped their arms back and forth. Then they got sarcastic, which was fun to watch. They do-si-doed. They tried the hornpipe. They did a dangerous love train that kept crashing into everyone because they were blotto. He got behind her and waved his hands and she waved her hands like cobras and she sung out, "Do the Vishnu!" I was jealous. It looked like fun. I could picture Diana and I dancing. Cutting the rug. That's the saying.

"Hey, man," I said. "You two Vishnu like fiends."

"You want to dance?" Jenn asked. She rubbed her wet hair back out of her face.

"Thanks," I said. "Not right now. I've got something on my mind." I asked Rick, "Can we talk?"

He nodded. "I'll be right back," he said to Jenn.

"I'll be missing you, hula-breath."

"I'll be missing you too, corker-dog."

"There will be a big empty place where you ought to be."

They blew kisses. They parted. Rick walked with me over to the coolers. There were Old Milwaukees and Cokes in ice. I dug for Coke. I popped the top, and we went off to the side.

"Man, am I in love with her," he said. "Sometimes it hurts."

"That's great," I said.

"Isn't she hot?"

"She is."

He nodded. "Damn straight."

I sipped my Coke. We sat on a rock. Our legs dangled. I wiped my mouth. Rick kicked his heels against the stone. He turned his head toward me.

"So what's the skinny?"

"Here's the deal. I want to move in on Stacey."

"Turner's girlfriend?"

"I think I really like her," I said. It was only half a lie. I liked her sort of.

"That's great. You like her."

"She's cool."

"You are one dumb sap."

"She's been flirting."

"He'll toast you, boy. He's done it before."

"Look, Rick. This is embarrassing: I need advice."

"Try 'run away.' "

"On how to get her to make out."

"What are we talking here?"

"Maybe like second or third base or something."

"Could you not use a softball metaphor around me? In fact, could you never mention softball again in my presence?"

"Rick. I need advice. She doesn't think I'm normal enough."

"I can't think why. Maybe because you're one weird-ass freak."

"Just tell me how. If I can carry off normal for an hour or so, she's mine."

"It's your funeral, bud."

"Rick," I pleaded, trying to make my eyes as large and watery as possible. "I'm asking you a favor. You know all about this love stuff. I really, really like her. You know, I looked across that fire and thought, *She's the one. I need her.* Being near you and Jenn, I see what that can be like, when you find that one right person. It could be love. What I'm asking you is to tell me how to win her heart."

"Really? You really into her?"

"I am," I said earnestly. "Wicked."

Rick looked serious. "Okay, man. There's only one secret. It isn't too tough."

"Yeah?"

"It's kind of embarrassing."

"Shoot."

"Get her drunk. It lowers the inhibitions."

I stared at him. "That's your advice? You? Dr. Love? Get her drunk?"

"Come to think of it, more important, you'd better get yourself drunk too. You have a little inhibition problem."

"That's the secret of love? Get both of us blitzed and start feeling her up?"

"Well, she'll start feeling you up too," he said in his defense. "It's not that bad. You'll both be really confused and won't care. Honestly, man. That's how Jenn and I got together."

"You kidding?"

"I can't even remember it. At some point I remember

reaching up her shirt. My nose was running and I used the shirt to wipe it." He slid off the rock. He was on his feet. "Sometimes love needs a little push," he said. He jerked his head toward Jenn. "Come on," he said. "Let's go back."

We went back. Turner and some of the other guys were holding a boob-size contest. They ran back and forth with their hands outstretched and joined at the thumbs for measurement. "She's out, man! Out!" they shouted to each other. "Itsy-bitsy teeny-weenie." People around them crowed and clapped. Sometimes the girls laughed nervously. I watched Stacey. She smiled weakly when one of the boys came near her to measure. Then she went back to staring at the dirt. She was piercing a styrofoam plate with a fork again and again.

We found Jenn sitting by the edge of the fire. Rick said, "Hey there, woojy-coojy."

"Hi, moo-moo froo-froo."

"Liggly-giggly."

"Ploodle-woodle."

"Fubb-fubb-sudubb."

The party was in full swing. Two guys were fighting. They couldn't stand. One punched and sagged. The other pushed and fell. No one could tell what it was about. Kids circled them and shouted. The keg was empty. Guys were breaking out six-packs from the ice. Just outside the firelight, couples were grinding on the ground. Rick's brother sat among them as their hands rose and fell. He was on a stump, curled like a fetus, with his head jammed between his knees. His hands gripped his hair and kept twitching. All around him on the ground, they writhed. Their shorts were skewed. One girl was lying on top of a guy, her hands gripping his arms, her neck craned so she could take in her mouth another guy's toe. The rest of his foot was padded with dirt. He had grabbed some girl's hair. His mouth was open and he prayed silent words. Above them, Rick's brother rocked from side to side.

It was a completely repulsive scene. It was going to take a lot of Old Milwaukee before I could join in with anything like gusto. People were spinning in circles. People were kicking shrubs. A boy's shirt was wet with vomit that was not his own. The seventies leftovers were playing tom-toms and didgeridoos. One sang, "Your dreams are ours. Your dreams are ours. At O'Dermott's." And they all laughed. Someone had brought a kite.

"People!" said Turner. "People!" He clapped his hands. "Yo! Shut up!"

The music stopped. People looked up.

Turner was standing in the middle of the circle, near the fire. His hands were clasped behind his back. He was trying to be serious. His eyes were half-closed, and his face was red. "I think we should now take just a moment to . . . for a toast. I believe we should toast the corporation that made tonight possible."

There were a few cheers and whoops from around the fire.

And then I heard it. Farther off. Way beyond the bounds of the firelight. Down the hill, in the woods.

Someone else whooping. Many people. Distantly.

I looked quickly at Shunt. He was standing alone by the other side of the fire. He nodded at me.

Turner hadn't noticed. He kept on talking. "O'Dermott's is an American institution. It's as American as . . ." He thought for a second. He was getting tears in his eyes. He was drunk. "It's as American as the open road. It's as American as freedom. It's like driving across the highways of this country with your roof down. I love you guys. You're my coworkers. I love you. We're part of something big. You drive across the country, where there are like . . . what are those called? Those tall . . ." He made a sign with his hand.

People tried, "Silos?"

"Mesas?"

"Rockets?"

Nobody noticed the sound of a distant engine in the woods, where no engine should have been.

"Last year, I'm driving across the country. Everywhere I look, I see O'Dermott's. Sometimes in the middle of a field. Sometimes on a cliff over the sea. That's what America is about, man. It's about big. It's about the open road. It's about exploring, like . . . you know, those explorers. It's about a big new country that's always getting bigger. It's about," he cried, raising his beer toward heaven, "the emerald oval stretching from the mountains to the prairies, to the oceans wet with foam. To O'Der—"

In the dark woods, there was a splash too loud to ignore. Turner stopped. He said, "Wha?"

Shunt stepped into the ring. It was time to create a diversion. "Freedom?" he said loudly. There was another distant cheer far off in the darkness. Turner blinked. Shunt yelled, "I'll tell you about freedom! Hey, Turner!" Turner stumbled to face him. Shunt said as noisily as he could, "I'll tell you about freedom! Cattle in a cycle of continuous forced pregnancies until they're killed for meat. Animals living their lives in boxes no larger than their bodies. Where's freedom there? Where is it? I'm talking about the simple freedom," he said, pounding one hand on the other, "to make a ninety-degree turn once in your life! To turn like this! Animals who never once in their lives *turn around! Where's the freedom there?* I ask you—where's the freedom in advertising that—"

"Shut up," said Turner. He was listening hard to the forest. He waved his hand impatiently at Shunt.

"Freedom in advertising aimed to get kids—"

"Shut up! I said, shut up!"

People were sitting up. Couples stopped holding on to each other. People were blinking.

"Look," said Shunt, throwing himself in Turner's way. "I'm talking about artificial ingredients that make us the most obese nation in the world!"

Turner shoved him to the side. Turner was headed out of the ring of light. "What was that?" he said. "What was that?"

People peered into the darkness of the forest. People were following him. There was a long silence. We could hear his footsteps on leaves and sticks. They got softer. They faded away completely.

Then suddenly, "Oh my God!" we heard him sob. "Oh my God!"

We started running down the hill after him. We were a

big group. Branches snapped and cracked. We hurtled through the woods. The fire cast our shadows in front of us. I saw pale flashes of bark. We jumped over someone who'd passed out. It felt good, the night breeze whipping through my hair. The air against my ankles. Running with a crowd. Our feet flying through leaves.

"What is it?" someone yelled. And another: "I can't see! I can't see!"

I felt confident. I knew it was all working out. I laughed as I ran. *Now, Turner, let's see what you're made of. Let's see who's laughing now.*

People tripped and fell, got up and ran. People hollered advice without meaning. People yelled that they were lost. People scrambled in the pines. We were one big mob. I could feel the excitement. We poured out of the woods, between our cars.

Turner wasn't there.

He was down by the pond. He stood there with his hands on his head. I almost laughed again. He was standing by his car.

The car was door-deep in water.

The back was higher than the front. The engine was almost submerged. Even from where I was standing, I could see the pleather of the roof was slashed. There was writing in the paint.

I was not surprised. I hadn't known exactly what the BQ crew would do, but I'd had my suspicions. They'd gotten an anonymous call. It said that Turner had stolen the troll. It told them where to find it. Here, in his car, the night of this party. I'd growled, "You don't get here soon enough, and we're burning it in effigy."

They'd gotten here soon enough. The troll-shaped promotional condiment dump had been sitting in the back seat of Turner's car. Shunt and I had left it there.

So what had they done? I was proud of them. They had removed the troll. They had drowned the car. I suspected they'd pushed it with a truck. They'd keyed the paint job. They'd scratched:

CYRIL SUCKS

A DUMP FOR A DUMP

on the doors. And they didn't lie. In the back seat, where the troll had sat, they had left a dump. It must have been several people's. You could tell it was a BQ dump. O'Dermott's doesn't serve onion rings.

I didn't know whether to be impressed or disgusted. It was so completely disgusting it was almost impressive.

Turner had fallen to one knee. The other knee couldn't decide whether it was standing or sitting. It tried to straighten. It made him hop. He made a strange noise which I guess could be called a baying. He started to pound the dirt with his fists. At first it was left, right, left, right, left-right-left-right-left-right slamming the earth, and then together. Again. Again. Again. Again.

It felt very good. It was like someone had taken my heart and smeared it with a lotion smooth and cool.

Turner rose to his feet. He was slumped like a Neanderthal. He waded out beside his car. The water got deeper and deeper. It was up to his thighs. The picture was touching. He caressed the finish. He bent down low and whispered tearful things.

We all stood and watched. The moon was high above the pond. The trees were black. Things flew overhead.

Shunt muttered, loud enough for everyone to hear, "Bet it was those BQ bastards."

A couple of guys started to murmur. One called out to Turner, "Hey, Turner. Shunt said he thinks it was the BQ guys."

Turner looked up. He nodded fiercely.

With hard, strong strides he plowed out of the water. His hands were clenched. He stood on the shore. Water ran from him.

He cupped his hands around his mouth. His arms were thick with tension and muscle. He yelled into the darkness, "You listening? We're gonna whip your flame-broiled asses! You hear? I'm gonna personally claw out your throats and *eat 'em to go!*" He looked at all of us. "You in with me? Are you in with me? Don't just stand there, peckerheads! *It's time for violence!*"

He reached into his back pocket. He pulled out a Swiss Army knife. He unfolded the blade. He held it different ways in the moon to make it glint. He held out his hand.

Someone stepped forward and handed him something. He held it in his other hand. He raised the knife up. It was like he was performing a sacrifice. The knife came down.

He'd punctured the can of beer. He put it up to his

mouth. Popped the top. The shook-up beer started to squirt. He clamped his lips around the spray. He was shotgunning. He hardly missed a drop.

When it was done, he tossed the can aside. He wiped his mouth with the back of his hand. He let out a sigh.

Then he folded the knife. He put it back in his pocket. He smacked his fist into his hand. He and several of the guys went into war council.

Some people wanted to go back up to the fire. They were worried about the darkness. Others wanted to hunt the BQ crew down like pigs. Nobody wanted to leave. Who would want to miss the action?

"We have flashlights!" Turner yelled to everyone. "You want to join the fray, hook up with one of the light guys. We'll form posses. Search the woods. There are five cars which will give chase, in case they're already out of the woods. The rest of you, stick to the paths. Search high and low. When you find them, here's the plan: Beat the shit out of them. Make them scream. If you can, record it so I can hear."

People waved flashlights in the air. "Flashlight!" they sang. "Flashlight here." "I'm going over toward the river." "I'm going over toward the field." People collected in groups. There was a rustling all around us as posses headed off into the woods. We could hear branches snap. Cars were turned on. Headlights shot out across the water. They picked out bugs in the air. There was a clamor of three-point turns. The rattle of suspensions on washboard dips and bumps.

Turner's posses were spreading out. He looked

savage with anger. He banged a square red flashlight on the hood of a truck. His thumb hit the nubbin. The light went on.

"Follow me! Follow me!" he screamed. A group of guys holding sticks and flashlights whooped. They followed him.

We could hear underbrush torn and stomped on. Instructions hooted through the woods. Catcalls to summon. The honking of horns. The forest was alive. Soon, the clearing at the bottom of the hill was almost empty.

I went down by Turner's car. There was a small group of kids there. They were looking at the damage. They said, "Wow," and, "Whoa." One said, "Man."

Stacey was there. She was craning her neck. Looking into the back seat. Sniffing.

I stood next to her and made a show of trying to see the mess. "Here," I said. "Steady me." I grabbed her arm. I leaned far out over the water, leaning my hand on the car. With the other hand, I held hers. In the back seat, the heavy brown coils were just above the level of lapping water. One low dollop was disintegrating.

"What's it look like?" she said.

"Pull me back," I said. "It's pretty solid stool."

"Good," she said. "It serves the bastard right."

The little group was breaking up. The others were wandering away. They shook their heads.

Stacey and I were alone in the night. We could hear the distant hunting calls. "Another beer?" I offered.

Soon we were sitting by the pond on roots and drinking. Trees hung far out over the water. I felt relaxed.

Triumphant. Nothing was going to take away my victory now. She was almost mine. We talked. I tried to concentrate on her body. I checked out its length and excellence. The hair with its complications. When I ran my fingers through it, would it crackle with mousse? The face with just enough flesh that it would yield soft as warm butter when I kissed it.

Keep concentrating on the body, and how I want to bring it close to me. Forget about the rest. Don't make up scenes of anger afterward. Don't think about the things you'll have to say. Just think about desire. Her arms were silver in the moonlight.

I was consoling her.

"Can't believe he was scoring with that whore," she said.

"I know," I said softly, rubbing her arm with my hand. "He can be a real bastard."

"He can," she said. "Sure can."

We talked about his bastardry. I watched that she kept drinking.

"You're nice to talk to me," she said.

"No," I replied with a slim smile. "I'm not nice at all."

She raised an eyebrow. "I asked him about you," she said. "He called you bendy-boy. Why's that?"

I stopped the rubbing on her arm. "Because," I replied, "I'm a contortionist. You know. I can bend myself into the most amazing positions." I built up pressure in my fingers, gripped the muscle, squeezed. She was swaying toward me.

"Want to go in the water?" I asked, taking my hand away.

"Swimming?"

"Let's search the car." I rose and unbuttoned my shirt. "I'm going in," I said. "Come along?"

The night was warm. When I took off my pants, the air wasn't uncomfortable. I stood in my boxers. My toes were wound in the moss. I crossed my arms on my chest. My own bare skin on my skin felt good. She undressed in front of me. She left on her T.

The first shock of the water numbed my toes. Except at the very edge, where the mud was warm and soft, the water was chilled. We waded in together. When one of us tripped, we'd grab the other's flexing fingers.

And I thought to myself, *Baby's play*. She was mine. I flexed my toes in the soft mud as if discovering new muscles.

My legs prickled with the cold. I could feel the hairs standing stiff. Pulpy weeds sucked my calves. I turned to look at her. She was breathing deeply with the chill. The water was wetting the belly of her shirt. Her eyes were closed. I could smell the stench of beer.

I led her to the car. I climbed through the driver's window. I sat in the driver's seat. She was laughing. She was trying to clamber over the passenger's door.

"One sec," I said. Something was floating on her seat. I reached down and pulled it from the water. "Look," I said, with a smile. "His O'Dermott's jacket."

The green sateen looked almost black, it was so wet. The elastic cuffs sagged.

"I hate that goddamn jacket," she said. "It is so . . . it

is so . . . I don't know." She blew out some air between her lips and made them sputter. She tried again to climb the door. She almost fell. I was worried she would bark her shin. I quickly reached up to take her hands.

We were sitting side by side. I draped the green sateen jacket around her shoulders.

Now, Turner, I thought. *This is it. I'm taking what you took and more. There's nothing left of you.*

Water bugs skated between us, rebounded off the dashboard. Their dimples on the water were bright with reflection.

Okay, I thought. *Now what? The final touch.*

We sat in the silent car, our limbs so numb they were like blue marble. The pond was like a road before us. The moon was high.

"Where—where do you want to go?" I asked, and put my arm around her shoulders. The cold sateen clung to my skin.

"Don't know," she said sloppily.

"This," I said, "is like a drive-in for salamanders." And somehow I realized: That's all I need to say. I can kiss her now. Water wandered in and out of my boxers. It was like they weren't there. My legs were numb, but I could feel the upholstery intimately against my butt. As if I were nude. My parts were moving in currents of their own.

Ignore what you're about to do. If you're happy and so's she, what's it matter? Look at the body. Look at it now.

There is a certain ferocity you need, to be a teenager in America.

I moved toward her. I put my arms on either side of

her. She put her arms around my neck. She pulled me toward her. My neck kinked. I was briefly worried about whiplash. That would look really bad, in a submerged vehicle. I pressed up against her beer-smelly mouth. We ate at each other's lips. We were locked around each other. Her leg went up. She bit my tongue. I swore. She slurred, "Sorry," and we were back clenching. Triumph. *Got you, Turner. Got you.* I ran my hand under the green sateen jacket. Like a fish slipped under her shirt. Moving my mouth against her face. Her eyes closed. The reek of beer and BQ dump. The sleekness of her skin. The trickle of water from our limbs. The slosh of passenger-side pond.

And suddenly, a crash by the shore.

I shot straight up. I stood. The car lurched. I steadied myself on the door.

Looked around. Couldn't see a thing. The moon. The water. Shadows.

Someone moving.

Someone was in the water. They were watching us. There was a splashing.

"Oh God," said Stacey. She was hunching. "Oh God, I'm dead. I'm like so dead."

I swore, and tumbled out of the car. I fell into the water ungracefully. My arms were out. They hit the weedy bottom. I rose and spit out pond.

"Who is it? Who's that?" Stacey hissed to me.

I squinted. There was another splashing near an oak.

He came out into the light. He was rubbing his arms so hard it looked like the skin would come off. His mouth was in a grimace.

"It's Rick Piccone's brother," I told her. "Do you know Rick Piccone?"

"No," she said. "What the hell's he doing?"

"Hey!" I said to Rick's brother. "Hey, there! It's Anthony! Rick's friend?"

He moaned. He scrubbed.

I walked toward him.

"Hey, man," I said. "Like, you okay?"

He was shivering with the cold. His teeth were chattering. Still he kept scrubbing. He wouldn't look at me. He kept saying, "Vuhvuhvuhvuhvuhvuhvuhvuh," in rhythm with his shivers.

"You okay?" I repeated. I was by his side. I grabbed his arms and tried to lift him up. He was freezing. He was naked. He stayed squatting.

"No. Not okay." He shook his head like a piece of wood.

"What's the matter?"

"I thought I could clean myself," he wept. "But I'm not just dirty. I'm actually dirt. We're all just dirt."

"Come on," I said gently. "I'll take you home."

"Never," he said, and slapped at me. "Never. Their idea of clean is chemicals. That's what happens to linoleum." His voice was getting higher and higher. "We're all crumbly. My arms and belly are washing away."

I dragged him toward the shore. He was shaking his head. Again and again he repeated, "Nothing is right. Look around you. Look around. Nothing is right. Nothing is right anymore."

"What's wrong with him?" said Stacey.

"Nothing is right. Look around you. Nothing is right anymore."

"Whose brother is he? What circus did he escape from?"

"I've got to take him home," I said.

"Not home. Not home. 'Put a sock in it.' 'Put a sock in it.' Medications three times daily. Breakfast, lunch, and dinner."

"I guess this means we aren't going to do it," said Stacey.

I looked at the submerged car. I looked at her in the green sateen jacket. I looked at Rick's brother, shivering on the shore. I looked at my legs, streaked with mud and scum. I felt a sickness running all throughout me.

"Why bother?" I said to her. "Why bother, really? Now I'm as bad as Turner. Except that I'm a loser. This is stupid. Revenge. Idiotic. There's no point anymore."

"I don't know exactly what that means," said Stacey, "and I think I'm probably glad."

And again and again, what was going through my head was this: *This is not my victory. There is no victory for losers.*

We got dressed, and looked for Rick's brother's clothes in the bushes. He was standing near the car. We took his clothes back to him.

He was standing with his arms spread, looking up at the vast night sky. "The stars look small and clean," he said, and they were reflected in his tears. "But really they're just big galactic farts."

She and I got him dressed. "I'm sorry," I said to her. "I'm really sorry."

She nodded impatiently. "Whatever happens, everybody's really sorry," she said.

We walked him to my parents' car. I wrote a note for Rick. It was on lined notebook paper. I stuck it under his windshield wiper.

Up on the hill, a didgeridoo and guitar were playing "Feelings."

Chapter 7

· · · · · · · · · ·

Usually I walked to O'Dermott's. The next day I drove. I didn't have to go in. We were all off for the day. But I wanted to see the commercial get shot. I wanted to hear what had happened the night before.

As I drove along, I wondered nervously if whatever happened would be my fault. The insults, the paid-off umpire, the stolen drive-thru speaker—I hadn't done any of them. But they were all the result of me having stolen the troll. Maybe they would have happened anyway. I hadn't created the rivalry in the first place. Turner would have stolen the troll himself if he'd thought of it. He hated BQ. If he had stolen the troll, everything would have turned out just like it did. It wasn't really me who had destroyed his car.

What an idiot I was. I could have banged my head against the steering wheel, except most of it was the horn.

The O'Dermott's parking lot was full. I parked along the road. There were big trucks with cables. People had come from all around to see the cast and crew. There were mothers and daughters. There were old men and women. There were Cub Scouts. Turner was striding around like lord of the manor. He was followed by three friends who worked grill.

Rick and Jenn were there. They waved and I walked over. Rick said, "Thanks for taking my brother home last night."

"He okay?" I asked.

"I don't know," said Rick miserably.

"What happened after I left?"

"No one found the BQ crew," said Jenn. "Turner and a couple of other guys went and threw rocks through BQ's windows."

"There's a big thing about it in the paper," said Rick. "Look at these security guards."

Security guards were walking on the sidewalk, talking into walkie-talkies. They were drinking coffee. They were lighting each other's cigarettes.

They walked through the crowd, keeping an eye open. Occasionally, they'd say something like, "You'll have to remove the baby during the taping, ma'am." The crowd was held back by cones. Management had ordered their Staff to dress in white overalls and spear wrappers in the bushes. The Staff moved along slowly, raking the wood-chips after they passed. They were making everything tidy.

Suddenly, I spotted Diana. She was leaning against the wooden fence with some friends. She tossed back her hair with her hand. They weren't her BQ friends. I didn't recognize them. Maybe they were visiting from out of town. I saw her flinch, and suddenly turn her face like she'd been hit. No. She was trying to hide.

She had seen Turner. She whispered something to one of her friends. They put their arms around her, one on each side, and they quickly walked away. I watched Turner. He hadn't seen them. He was talking to one of the film crew. I decided I better keep out of Turner's way, too. I went around the corner of the building. Spectators were setting up lawn chairs and settling in for the day. There were little kids crying to know when they'd meet Kermit O'Dermott. There were senior citizens trying to score coffee. There were men and women dressed in dentist's clothes.

Shunt was having a conversation with one of the guys from Management.

"What's your annual salary, sir? Rounding down?"

"Mike said you know where the paper goods are kept."

"Just tell me your salary. I'm curious."

"Could you get me one of those packets of napkins?"

"Here's what I'm wondering: I'll bet you make at least five or six times what I make in a year—"

"You know, those refill packets for the dispensers?"

"—and yet, and yet, you don't have to put up with the noise, the constant shouting, the grease, the all-day idiocy of the condiment routine, the uncertain hours, the bitching, the monotony, the constant standing, the heat of the grill for ten, sometimes eleven hours."

"Mike said you know where the napkins are kept."

"I guess what I'm saying is I'm wondering why I'm getting minimum wage for a job that is more dangerous, more monotonous, and closer to the customer than yours is."

"We need these dispensers to be full."

"If my job is more difficult, shouldn't I get paid more instead of less?"

"Look. I'm paid for my expertise. I'm paid to think. You're paid to work manually. I'm like the brain and you're like the muscle. There's no better or worse. We work together. Now. Napkins?"

"But I actually think a lot when I'm on the job. I'm thinking all the time."

"Could you get me one of the packets they use to refill the dispensers?"

"Would you say that my brain is an unnecessary byproduct? Would that be fair?"

"You must have a supply closet somewhere."

"Would you sell my brain if you could? For a profit?"

"Look, fine. I'll get my own goddamn napkins. Thanks for nothing, kid."

Someone somewhere was talking into a loudspeaker. I couldn't hear the words. A truck was backing into the driveway, beeping. People scattered away from it. I couldn't see what was happening inside the building. There were flashes of light in the windows. I went around the corner.

A path to a side door surrounded by shrubs and wood-chips had been marked off with yellow tape. They were getting ready to film a scene there. People were crowded up against the tape, watching.

Some of the guys from BQ were standing near a split-rail fence. I recognized Johnny Fletcher and Kid. Johnny dribbled a Coke can between his feet. Kid passed out pieces of grape Bubblicious.

Cameras were set up in the parking lot. Two girls in blue polyester graduation gowns were being coached. A man yelled at them, "Keep thinking: This is the first day of the rest of my life!" They were supposed to be laughing and stumbling out of the glass doors. In one hand they held their mortarboards. In the other they held O'Dermott's bags. A prop man was filling up the bags with more paper. I guess he didn't fill them with real food because the grease might bleed. I watched the girls put out their cigarettes and, after one coughed a few times, they suddenly were happy. They jostled each other. They practiced throwing their mortarboards up in the air. The director asked if they could get more spin. The prop guy came out and I could see him showing them a wrist action. The yellow tape rippled in the breeze. The director yelled that he wanted to try a take. One of the girls yelled back that she still didn't get it with the mortarboards, was it overhand or underhand. The other one yelled that she had a migraine.

Suddenly I felt someone at my elbow. My co-conspirator.

"Top o' the morning," said Shunt.

"It went off great," I said.

"We rule."

"I'm feeling kind of guilty."

"Guilt's for the weak."

"A lot of damage has been done."

"To multinational corporations. Cry me a river."

"No, not that. More Turner. I feel like I became what I hate most. But a clumsy, stupid version."

"Heads up."

"Hm? I'm saying I think my greatest enemy was really myself."

"Heads up."

"It was stupid, what I did to Turner."

"Um, enjoy the ride," Shunt said, and stepped backward.

Someone grabbed my neck. My shoulders hunched. A voice said near my ear, "Hey, bendy-boy. How's my girlfriend?"

"Turner!" I choked.

"I heard about everything. You have made a really, really big mistake."

"A really big mistake," echoed one of his friends.

He shoved me hard. I staggered and almost fell. I caught myself and stood.

"I'm gonna beat you so hard, crap's gonna come out your nose and ears."

"Turner—" I said.

But it was a fight. There was nothing I could do. I tried to think of something funny to say, but there wasn't time. His friends were clearing room. He was putting up his fists. He had a stance.

I saw faces collecting around us. I heard shouts. The director was screaming at us. Then the first fist fell. It slammed across my cheek like nothing I'd ever felt. I couldn't breathe. I reeled. I tried swinging. Nothing there. Another punch in the gut. I choked. I gagged. I bent over. Everything else, that had just been bully fighting. This was the real thing.

He wanted blood.

I stood. He was waiting. I shot toward him, hit his arm. Didn't even faze him. He grabbed my wrist. With the other fist, slammed me full in the face. My head shot back. Fresh feeling all across my nose. Numbness. Blood. My neck was what hurt. Lips buzzing.

He was holding me up. My legs limp. Arm wrenched. Diana's face, mouth open.

He pummeled my trunk. I felt the knuckles in the ribs. Little blasts of pain. Blood on my shirt. Stumbled back against the tape. Snapped it. Slapped at him. Felt the contact with his cheek. His head hardly budged.

He threw me down.

The voice of Kid—"Hey, Turner!"—voice of Fletcher—"Turner! Payback!"—Turner yelling something at them.

Rage as I lay there. Saw Turner's work boots, big and stupid. Grabbed his ankles. Yanked. He fell.

Wrestling. Now I got his neck. A hold. My contortion paying off. He gasped. His head in my locked arms. Banged it again and again against the pavement. Him blinking. His neck in my hands. Thumbs jabbing the throat. Kid and Fletcher looming.

Knee in my groin. Saw stars. Black ones glittering. Fell to the side. Smelled the grass. Freshly mown. Fletcher's heel whacking my gut. Turner yanking away from Kid on the ground. Clawing toward me. Fletcher's heel. My ribs.

Anytime, I thought. *Anytime, just let me pass out.* I couldn't take it anymore.

Fingers holding my chin. Felt his forehead slam mine. Turner. Head butt. Held me steady. Slammed again. *I'm going.* Held me steady. Slammed again. *Going.* Held. Slammed. *Gone.*

And there was a voice from above us on high that said, "No. Stop. What is the meaning of this?"

I started to breathe again. He didn't move. They didn't move. My eyes were closed. I smelled my steely blood.

And the voice above us spoke again, saying, "Stop fighting right now."

And I opened my eyes to see who it had come from; I opened them to see before me, toes turned up, the massive elfin shoes of Kermit O'Dermott.

He towered above us, looking down. His face was a face of anger. He didn't have his harp, with which he would often charm the fries to dance. He said to us, lying before him, "Order must be restored."

And Management came behind him. They were clothed in dark suits. They spoke, giving directions, and said to their Staff, "Pick them up. Get security over here. Send these boys on their way."

Their paid servants came, clothed in white. They extended their hands to us. They picked us up from the earth. They set us on our feet.

I could hear Shunt proclaiming loudly to reporters, "Gentlemen, I think I speak for myself and other upstanding suburbanites when I declare emphatically that this goes beyond the limits of healthy competition.

That's Cyril with a *C*, Einstein. And I think the dazed, anemic-looking kid's named Anthony something. Sirs, I'm all for a free market, but when it becomes violent in a way which disrupts my hard-earned bourgeois spending patterns, I know things have gone too far. Everyone in town thinks that's what's happened here between these two brutal franchises, and though I know none of the participants personally, frankly the whole sordid scene shocks me—shocks me!—as a responsible citizen just trying to do my job peacefully and occasionally purchase some animal flesh soldered into disks by cash-hungry imperialists. You getting all this?"

Rick and Jenn were on either side of me. "My God," Jenn was saying. "My God, my God. Are you hurt?"

"Thanks, guys," I said. My nose and mouth were stinging. I could feel them starting to puff. I was wet with blood. My head hurt badly.

Diana was standing in front of me. I tried to smile with my broken lips. I held my scarecrow arms out to her. "Diana," I said. "Diana." I loved the name, and wanted to repeat it. "Diana," I said warmly, "I did this all for you."

"I know," she said. "You really are an idiot."

"You've seen me only in the getting beaten up parts. But really, I—"

"Do I want to know? No. I'm telling you, you're an idiot."

"Everything I've done, I did because I love you."

"You really think I'm going to be flattered by this? Think about it, Anthony."

"Diana, I was getting revenge. I couldn't stand that he'd stolen you."

She jabbed her finger into my chest. Rick and Jenn followed it with their eyes. "That's exactly the problem," she said. "Did you ever think about this, Anthony: Turner didn't steal me. I'm not a piece of furniture. I went to him. It may have been stupid. It was stupid. But that was my choice."

"But when I felt so—"

"Listen. He didn't take me. It's not between you and him. It was my choice. And I'm finished with both of you. This is gross. This is totally repulsive. You are both completely pathetic."

And with that, she left.

"Diana?" I whined.

"Buck up, pal," said Shunt. "The hemorrhaging will stop eventually."

He looked grim, but satisfied. He was watching the elf.

"Well," he said. "Mission accomplished."

I shook my head. "I'm sorry, Shunt," I said. "I used the cause to get back at Turner. That's what it was really about."

"Don't sweat it. I knew you thought that's what it was about. But it wasn't about you or your problems. They're tiny. It was all for the cause. Disrupt the filming. Show people the fangs behind the bright O'Dermott's smile. Stir up local indignation. I thought it was pretty likely there'd be a high-profile fistfight today on camera between Turner and either you or me. Glad it was you. I took the liberty of inviting our friends from BQ. Anything to discredit the system."

We watched Diana and her friends get into a car. They drove off. She looked sorry for everything. Everything in the world.

"I loved her," I said.

Shunt gave me a weak smile. He looked down at the ground. It was the first time I had ever seen him look nervous. He looked back at me. He said, "Love is just a myth made up by the middle class to convince themselves they have an inner life. To convince themselves they're more than the meat they eat." He looked fiercer and more vulnerable than I had ever seen him look. "See you, man," he said. "I follow elf-boy wherever he goes."

With that, he dodged off into the crowd.

"Geez," joked Jenn, to break the silence once he'd gone, "I wonder what was eating him."

Rick and I looked at Jenn. Rick rolled his eyes. It was pretty funny. We all had to laugh.

After that, some executives scolded me. They told me I was fired. Turner was led past me. He hissed that he knew where I lived. I went inside with some men in suits. I signed some papers. The executives sat on two corners of a table and explained to me, one after the other, that I would not return to the premises, and that my final paycheck would be sent in the mail.

They gave me a form in triplicate. They said, "Read this and sign."

I stared at the page. They stood apart from me and whispered. I tried to read my paper. I couldn't read it. I felt dazed. I lifted up my hand. A lot of the skin was scraped off. I looked back at the page. One of the men was whispering to the other, "Can you tell me what the hell kind of manager runs a place like this?"

"I agree, Dave. This is unacceptable."

"I found the manager's copy of the ad script." The guy took a folded piece of paper out of his suit pocket. Unfolding it, he said, "It's covered with these . . . with this . . . this gross . . ." He scratched at the paper with his fingertips, speechless.

"Writing?" the other one suggested.

"This gross writing. All over it. It's like it was written by some kind of . . ."

"Some kind of animal."

"Yes. But what kind of animal would write this? You know? Does the manager find this funny?"

"Get him in here. Mike or whatever his name is. Tell him—"

"I'm ready," I called. They stopped whispering and both turned to look at me.

They came and took my papers. They didn't thank me for signing.

Then security guards led me to my parents' car. They watched while I opened the door. Jenn had cleaned the blood off my face. I wanted to get out of there. My nose and lips were huge. I wanted to clear my head.

I was free. No more revenge. No more O'Dermott's. I rolled up the windows, feeling good about myself. The hollering between Turner and the BQ crew got quieter as the glass slid up. I could hardly hear their threats anymore—Turner saying he was going to find out where they lived, Kid saying he already knew where Turner lived, Fletcher saying he didn't know where anybody lived and they should all just break bottles and settle it right there. I did a four-point turn and left the parking lot.

I drove to the woods, and got out to go for a walk. I locked the doors, and set off up the hill. Insects swarmed in the light. I felt good about myself for the first time in months. Completely good. I'd left the smell of grease behind me forever. I headed along the path, limping toward the sunlight and trees.

By the river, redwing blackbirds were darting through the reeds. I felt a real lightness through all my body. It was not just the blood loss. I was through. Through with all of it.

The forest seemed full of beauty that day. It smelled as fresh and clean as laundry detergent. The sun shone down on pines and oaks. Hubcaps full of bullet-holes were hung on trees like artwork. Cicadas buzzed in the leaves. Their voices rose and fell. Vines and creepers were growing up the "For Sale" signs on the houses across the river.

I sat and thought about my future. *So much for Diana*, I thought. *I really was an idiot.*

And later, as the sun picked out the yellow industrial foam on the riverbanks and made it shine like some froth of gold, I told myself, *After all, there are other fish in the sea.*

Epilogue ^TO GO
. . . .

About six months later, during Christmas break, I was loafing in Billingston's new Starbucks. I was waiting for Rick. We were going to talk about the latest girl who'd told me she wanted to just be friends. Rick had broken up with Jenn about two weeks after the O'Dermott's incident. They had done it and then decided they never wanted to speak again. It was something about whether to rent *Moonstruck* or *Bordello of Blood*.

I was sitting there watching the door when I saw a businessman come in. He ordered four bottles of water. He popped one of them open and began sucking on it. At first I didn't recognize him. Then I was shocked. "Shunt?" I said.

He had short hair that was parted carefully on the side. He was wearing a nice sports jacket. His pants were pleated.

"Anthony! What's up?" he said. He came over to my table. He gave me a firm handshake and smiled.

"Shunt," I said. "What happened?"

He looked down at himself. "What do you mean? I turned my life around," he said. "I got my GED and enrolled in a business program. I'm on the road to success."

"What road is that? Shunt, what have you done?"

"Burger U.," he said. "O'Dermott's management training program. I live in New Jersey now. Nice little apartment. Very comfortable."

I stood up. I couldn't sit any longer. "Good God!" I demanded, "Where did they put the implant?"

"Calm down, booj-boy. I'm an infiltrator. My Mr. Normal sports jacket has an orange and purple lining."

"Thank God," I said, and slumped back into my chair.

"I'm going to give you my card," said Shunt. "I want you for the Resistance."

"What are you doing here?" I asked.

"Going to stop at my folks'. "

"That's nice," I said. "Home for the holidays."

"Yeah. Just long enough to piss 'Merry X-mas' in the snow on the front lawn. Hence the four waters. I'm out of here."

He handed me a card. He waved and said, "Good to see you!" He raised two fingers, the pinkie and the pointer, as if he were about to make the "rave on" sign. Instead, he put them next to his head like a phone and jiggled them.

"Give me a ring sometime," he said, heading out the door. And just before it closed pneumatically: "We'll do lunch."

New York Times Bestsellers!

A NATIONAL BOOK AWARD WINNER

A MICHAEL L. PRINTZ HONOR BOOK

The Astonishing Life of Octavian Nothing,
Traitor to the Nation, Volume I: The Pox Party

Available in hardcover and paperback and as an e-book

A MICHAEL L. PRINTZ HONOR BOOK

The Astonishing Life of Octavian Nothing,
Traitor to the Nation, Volume II:
The Kingdom on the Waves

Available in hardcover and paperback and as an e-book

"Octavian Nothing's story encompasses both the
comic and the tragic with sweeping ambition."
— *The New York Times*

www.candlewick.com

MORE FROM M. T. ANDERSON

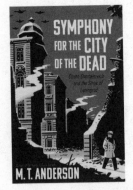